BLUE LIMBO

BLUE LIMBO

TERENCE M. GREEN

A TOM DOHERTY ASSOCIATES BOOK/NEW YORK

BLUE LIMBO

A Tor Book
Published by Tom Doherty Associates, Inc.
175 Fifth Avenue
New York, NY 10010

Tor Books on the World Wide Web:
http://www.tor.com

Tor® is a registered trademark of Tom Doherty Associates, Inc.

Design by Lynn Newmark

Library of Congress Cataloging-in-Publication Data

Green, Terence M.
    Blue limbo / Terence M. Green. —1st ed.
        p.   cm.
    "A Tom Doherty Associates book."
    ISBN 0–312–86282–2 (alk. paper)
    I. Title.
PR9199.3.G7574B58   1997
813'.54—dc20   96–30648

First edition: January 1997

Printed in the United States of America

0 9 8 7 6 5 4 3 2 1

For my father
Thomas Matthew Green
1904–1995

ACKNOWLEDGMENTS

There are always behind-the-scenes readers and encouragers and advisers to whom I am grateful. This time around: Staff Sergeant Terry Adams of the Metro Toronto Police Force (55 division); great friends and great writers Rob Sawyer and Andrew Weiner; terrific supporters and readers Ken and Judy Luginbuhl, Bill and Judy Kaschuk, Tom Potter and Cindy Estabrooks, Doug Blake and Joe Belliveau; former agent and editors Carol Bonnett, Linda Williams, Lesley Choyce; the friendship and support of the East York C.I. English Department; the enthusiasm of Sunnybrook's Don Plewes (and Charlotte Danard), Stuart Foster, Mike Bronskill, and Mark Henkelman; and the wisdom and camaraderie of the collegiate *literati:* Gary Reilly, Greg Hughes, Don Hibbert, and Ron Whiteside.

Special thanks to my agent, Shawna McCarthy, and a double note of sincere thanks to David Hartwell—remarkable editor, remarkable man.

Merle, Conor, and Owen know how important they are to me and to my writing. But as always, I'd like it to be a matter of record: simply, they make it all worthwhile.

BLUE LIMBO

PROLOGUE

As the copter lost altitude, Mitch Helwig, encased inside the prototype Honda skimmer that hung below it, suspended on steel cables like a spider dangling from some nightmarish hummingbird, donned his night goggles. Then he tripped the switch on the dashboard radio, opening the line to the copter above.

The pilot's voice came out of the dashboard. "That's it, straight ahead."

Peering ahead and down into the rivers of light, Mitch finally made it out.

The warehouse. Herrington Storage.

"Got it."

It was big enough to provide the illusion of a small runway from the air. They dropped farther, staying well above the power lines, angling toward the long roof.

"I'll let you know when," said Mitch.

They dropped lower, still maintaining a steady forward motion. This must be, thought Mitch, what it's like to try to land on an aircraft carrier.

"Just don't signal for release if you figure you're more than eight or ten meters above the rooftop. Too dangerous."

"Right."

They were flying low over residential Leaside, the houses dark.

Maintaining speed.

Lower.

Lower.

Laird Drive.

Now.

He fired the skimmer's engines. They caught and idled.

"Release."

Mitch felt the clamps open, felt himself drop, then glide downward. He pumped the corner thrusters, waiting for the familiar ground-effect sensation, and angled the horizontal tail planes for maximum brakage. There was a moment of remote cold as he thought that it wasn't going to work—the instant between his adjustments and the tactile sensation of the skimmer's action upon the surface of the roof below him.

For a moment there was nothing.

He dropped.

Then he felt it, and relief flooded through him. It had taken hold. He was hovering.

He was down.

The Sikorsky HH–90B Blackhawk was already dwindling into the night, out across the Don Valley, before swinging around and heading back into the city. Mitch had to hope that any eyes on the ground, or within the warehouse, would have followed the copter's noise. Since the whole operation had transpired without visible lights, the hope was that the skimmer had not even been seen. And why would anyone have been looking for it? The operation he had just taken part in had been a first. They hadn't even been sure it would work.

But it *had* worked. And he was here—inside the security fence—having avoided detection. And hopefully, with a way out over the fence, once the job was done.

He cut the engines, and the skimmer settled onto the roof. Popping the door open, he let it float upward.

And he listened.

He heard what he wanted to hear: silence.

Stepping out into the night, he listened again. Still nothing.

Bending, he brought out the leather satchel from the floor behind the driver's seat, grasping it in his left hand. His right

hand reached into his duffle bag on the passenger seat and
withdrew the Bausch & Lomb hand-laser. Crouching, he ran
toward the nearest edge and peered down.
There was no activity. Nothing.
He pressed the light on his watch: 2:20 A.M. Reaching into
the satchel, he withdrew the twelve RDX bombs and placed
them carefully in a row on the roof in front of him, like a
mason examining a dozen imported bricks. Each one had been
set for a ten-minute countdown, once activated. All Mitch had
to do was press the buttons. After he'd told him what he needed
to do, Berenson, the force's mobile equipment manager, had assured him that these were what he wanted. RDX, Hexogen, T_4, Cyclonite—it went, he had been told, by several names. Plastic explosive, four times more powerful than any dynamite. Then Mitch reached into the satchel and withdrew the dozen plastic propane gas cylinders—each one about fifteen centimeters in length, shaped like bloated Polish sausages. *Gas-enhanced RDX,* he thought. It had been used to assassinate the Israeli prime minister last year.

He extracted the roll of adhesive tape from the satchel and spent the next two minutes carefully "bonding" each brick to its own cylinder. This done, he sat back on his haunches and breathed deeply.

For maximum effect, he knew they all had to go off within seconds of one another.

He checked his watch again: 2:25 A.M.

It was time.

As rhythmically as a clock ticking off the seconds, Mitch pressed the starter button on each of the dozen bombs in sequence, so that at 2:25:12 A.M. he had nine minutes and forty-eight seconds until they began to erupt, just as rhythmically.

His hands felt sweaty.

The digits on each bomb blinked away, counting off the seconds.

Mitch left the first one where it was, but gathered the others carefully into the satchel, stood up, and scanned the vast rooftop. Then he began to walk briskly, stopping and placing them in widely separated spots.

Six. Seven.

Another fifty meters. Eight. Nine.

Fifty more meters. Ten.

Then it happened.

The laser beam lit the night, slicing through the shoulder strap, burning through his jacket, his shirt, stopping only upon encountering the Silent Guard body armor. Mitch's hand darted for the broken strap of the bag, catching it before it could hit the roof and send him unceremoniously into eternity.

He made his decision at the same instant.

Lowering the satchel carefully to the roof, he clutched his shoulder as if he had been hit fully and slumped forward in feigned death.

For a minute there was no sound—nothing. Then, through the night goggles, he saw the torso of a man appear over the edge of the roof, hauling himself up via the rungs of a fixed metal ladder.

He waited until the man had stepped onto the roof before rolling quickly to one side and aiming his Bausch & Lomb. The needle of light flared to life, tracked onto the figure at the roof's edge. There was a muffled oath of anger and shock. The man slumped forward heavily on his face.

Mitch breathed in ragged gasps, all his senses alert. There was no doubt in his mind that the man was dead. The only question was whether or not he was alone.

He lay perfectly still. Listening. Watching.

Beside him, the digits ticked away relentlessly.

Satisfied that the man had been alone, Mitch sprang to a crouch and scuttled across the intervening space to see for himself. The man was lying face down. Mitch turned him over with a shove of his foot, bent, checked his pulse, then went to the ladder and peered down.

Empty.

A lone watchman, it seemed.

Then he checked his watch again: 2:31 A.M.

Christ.

Running back to the satchel, he carefully pulled out the remaining two bombs and hurried off to place them strategically.

He checked again: 2:32.

He broke into a run, heading back along the roof in the direction of the skimmer. The run took him the better part of a minute. Gasping, he swung himself into the driver's seat and fired the engines. They hummed into life and the skimmer rose up on its air cushion. Now, thought Mitch, we'll see whether this baby can leap tall buildings in a single bound. Because if she doesn't . . .

He ran it down the length of the roof as if he were preparing for takeoff at an airport. The roof's edge loomed rapidly closer.

Closer.

He pumped the corner thrusters and she leapt out into the void. He flipped the switches for full lighting. There could be no secrecy now. He had to know where the ground was. *Had to.*

He was coming down. About seven meters to go.

He angled the horizontals.

Yes . . . yes . . . there . . .

He had it! He could feel the ground. The skimmer's nose tilted forward awkwardly, scraping briefly along the asphalt, and then it righted itself and Mitch opened the throttle.

At the same time, three large field lights erupted to life, bathing the yard with glaring illumination.

Mitch accelerated across the yard, heading straight for the fence. It had been his intention to slow if possible and burn his way out with the skimmer's laser. But there was no time for that now. There was no time for anything.

He revved it to maximum. The skimmer screamed across the asphalt. When he got to within twenty meters of the fence, he pumped the corner thrusters with a sudden, wrenching spurt, then turned them on full, and the revs whined far past the red line as the skimmer rose off the ground, higher, higher, straining at three meters, groaning at four, shuddering violently at five—

—and then floated over the top of the fence, and angled down toward the ground, until it was back in touch with its normal physics and capabilities.

Mitch risked a glance at his watch: 2:34.

But how many seconds?

The skimmer was running full down Commercial Road when it began.

Mitch executed a horizontally sliding turn onto Laird as the second explosion went off. Then the blasts rocked the night at one-second intervals for the next ten seconds. At Eglinton Avenue, Mitch stopped, got out, and watched the volcano of orange and blue and white and red flames as they roiled upward, howling with crackling rage at the cold night sky, belching clouds of expanding, boiling black smoke with the fury of a sleeping giant suddenly awakened.

Within seconds, the night was alive with the sound of sirens. Karoulis, he thought, had kept them offstage nicely, until just the right moment.

ONE

We work in the dark—we do what we can—we give what we have. Our doubt is our passion and our passion is our task.

—Henry James
The Middle Years

1 "You're going to be suspended."

Mitch Helwig stared at his superior officer, Sam Karoulis, without expression.

It had been coming.

Still, when it came, he was surprised at how he felt: like a depth charge had been detonated nearby.

"I think I'm next," Karoulis added. "There's going to be a complete overhaul." He walked to his desk, took a cigarette from the top drawer.

Mitch watched, still silent.

"Not supposed to smoke these things in here, you know. Smoke-free zone." He struck a match on the cardboard package he took from the same drawer, held it to the cigarette's tip, inhaled deeply. He let the smoke expel slowly. "Fuck it," he said.

"Captain—"

"That's another thing," interrupted Karoulis. "There was even talk of going back to the way it used to be. Twentieth-century stuff. Superintendents, inspectors, constables . . . No more captains." He paused. After another deep draw on the cigarette, he met Mitch's eye. "They want me too."

"Names, titles, structures," Mitch said. "Big fucking deal. We know what's happening." He put his hands in his pockets.

Karoulis stared hard at Mitch. "Yes," he said. Then he nodded. "We do. Indeed, we do."

Mitch Helwig of the Toronto Police Force remembered it all.

All.

Mario. It had started when he had been killed. His partner, his best friend.

And with Karoulis's help, Mitch had ended it all. They had done what was necessary, used what was necessary, broken the rules.

But they had been right. And they had made a difference.

The Archangel was gone. Herrington Storage—the warehouse cover for it all—was gone. Closing his eyes, Mitch could see the flames blossom, smell the sulfurized smoke as it mushroomed into the darkness; he could still feel the explosions rocking him in his skimmer as the night swallowed him, drawing the poison from his heart.

Karoulis. The man had finally crossed the line to Mitch's side. The war could not have been won any other way. It had gone too far.

And now a new enemy. It was not over.

"Who?" Mitch asked. "Who's giving the order to suspend me?"

Karoulis met his eyes.

"Will it come from the top? From the chief of police?"

Karoulis shook his head. "Close, though," he said. "Galecki. He's the one."

Mitch was only mildly surprised. So, he thought. At last. One of the jackals steps from the shadows, sidles into the twilight. Joseph Galecki, one of the three deputy chiefs, was going to champion reform within the ranks, for his own dubious purposes.

Or was Mitch wrong? Was Galecki simply a bureaucrat?

"What do you think?" he asked Karoulis.

The captain shook his head. His eyes slid around the walls and ceiling of his office, deep in the core of Station 52 on Dundas Street, then back to Mitch's face. This, he implied, is no longer a place where such opinions should be aired. The world is more devious than we can imagine.

Mitch understood. He asked another question. "What do I do now?"

"You go home. You wait. I'll be in touch."

Go home, Mitch thought. Karoulis didn't know.

It was no longer that simple.

Huziak watched as Mitch Helwig left Karoulis's office. Everyone in the station, it seemed, could feel the vibrations—like aftershocks following the earthquake.

"Mitch."

Mitch turned to meet the face of the staff sergeant.

"You okay?"

Mitch nodded, smiled. "Thanks."

"What happened?"

Mitch was quiet for a moment, weighing words that he would never say. He studied the man behind the desk, listened to his somewhat asthmatic breathing, saw the buttons of his shirt pulled tight at the girth above his belt, and thought how he didn't know him as well as he should after so many years. Then he said, "I'm going to be suspended."

Neither of them said anything.

Mitch broke the silence. "What's new with you, champ?"

Huziak smiled softly. He shook his head, ran a hand through his thinning hair, and shrugged at the paperwork covering his desk. "All this stuff, I still got to wade through, and they want to take a good man like you out of service." He shrugged again. "Why don't they give you to me to use? I could use you." His hand passed over the clutter in front of him. "Help me clear up this stuff."

Unsure what to say, Mitch forced a smile again. "What's the big item today?"

"Big item," Huziak muttered. "Big fucking items." His big

hands shuffled through the papers. "First it's lasers. Now it's zappers."

Mitch watched him, half listening, half lost in the tangle of his own thoughts.

"Guy who manages three Swiss Chalets in the downtown core has just armed his entire staff with zappers." He held a sheet of paper at arm's length. "One of his waitresses complained—isn't sure it's legal." He looked up. "Or," he continued, "there's the betting pool we've uncovered, which tries to predict the date of Toronto's next police slaying. Vice searched a house in Parkdale, found about five hundred grams of marijuana, and a pool chart with several names and eight columns numbered one to thirty-one. What do you think of that one?"

"Christ."

"My sentiments exactly. Organized crime here and in the States nets more than two hundred billion dollars profit, costs more than seven hundred thousand jobs, is bigger than the paper, rubber, and tire industries, and we've got zappers in our Swiss Chalets. Guys are betting when we'll get iced. And they come down on guys like you in their never-ending battle against the Bad Guys. Go figure."

Huziak seemed to have gotten it all out. They said nothing for a few seconds.

"If I can do anything, Mitch . . . "

Mitch nodded. "Thanks. I just might have to take you up on it."

"What do you do now? Go home for a while?"

Without answering, Mitch turned his gaze very slightly toward the wall behind Huziak. His eyes focused on something very far away, something not in the room or the building, something he had lost and did not know how to find.

2 Phil Huziak waited fifteen minutes before taking in the morning's latest to Karoulis. He knocked gently. "Yes?"

Huziak opened the door slightly and stuck his round head in. "Me, Cap'n."

"Formal this morning, aren't we?"

"Saw Mitch coming out earlier."

Karoulis nodded. Even with his mind elsewhere, he understood the necessity of maintaining routines. "C'mon in."

Huziak ambled in. "You want to do this now?"

"Sure, sure. Sit down. It doesn't matter. Coffee?"

"Yeah. I'll get it." Huziak walked over to the ancient Mr. Coffee maker in the corner. There was still lots left in the carafe. "You too?"

"Thanks."

"Got one you'll like, Captain." He poured into two Styrofoam cups.

"I never shoot the messenger."

"Says you."

Karoulis smiled, weakly. "What is it?"

Huziak handed him his coffee and sat down. "Bomb squad cleared the bus station on Bay Street this morning. Six A.M. Ticking sound from a trash can spooked everybody."

"And I'm going to like this one?"

"Well, the squad's used to finding clocks and stuff, but

they tell me it's the first time they ever found an abandoned vibrator." He chuckled.

"Jesus."

"They were having a ball filling out the report when I came in this morning."

"Should get them through the day."

"And," Huziak hitched his pants over his stomach, rolled his eyes back in thought, "I've asked DeMarco, C.O.B., Homicide, to look into a rifle found wedged into a Goodwill box on Church Street. Some guy called last night. Was stuffin' clothes in and noticed it."

"What kind of a rifle?"

"Sanyo. Laser."

"Christ." No ballistics possible, he thought. As usual.

"We'll check it for prints. See if we can trace it."

They both knew it would most likely prove futile.

"And we picked up three teenagers last night. Tip came in. Frightening kids. We were able to lay sixty-four charges. One kid's charged with fifty-one counts of breaking, entering, and theft, four counts of robbery, and four counts of possession of stolen goods. They're responsible for dozens of break-ins, mostly in Riverdale. One of them had this on him." He reached in his pocket, took out what looked like a car key that had been honed to a point, and put it on Karoulis's desk.

Karoulis looked at it. "What is it?"

"A master key, for Japanese cars. It opens doors and starts ignitions as fast as the owner can with the proper key."

Karoulis had heard of them. Cars could be gone in thirty seconds. This was what was assumed to have been used in fifty percent of the thefts of Toyotas, Datsuns, Nissans, Mitsubishis, and Hondas in the greater metro area. It looked so simple, he thought. In the age of the microchip, everything could look so simple.

"I borrowed it from Evidence to show you. Thought you'd like to see one."

"Mmm." Karoulis held it at arm's length, thinking. It reminded him of something else he'd never seen. "The new zappers."

"What's that?"

"The new zappers. I've never seen one of them either."

"You're kidding. They aren't all that new."

"I'm a little slow sometimes, Huziak." He put the key down on the desk. "Sometimes I think it's all passing me by."

"I've got one tagged in my desk outside. Want to see it?"

"Sure." Karoulis started to get up.

"I'll get it, Captain. Don't get up."

"I want to get up. I'm a little restless."

Huziak smiled wryly, nodding. "Sure. C'mon." He led the way.

When they reached the desk, Huziak reached into a lower drawer and produced the item. Karoulis lifted it from his hand, turning it over curiously.

"That one's a Nova XR One Thousand. Weighs about two hundred grams. Uses a nine-volt battery. You hold it up against someone, it sends them sixty thousand volts. Manufacturers claim no permanent injury, unless you hold it against a person for several minutes. Stuns the muscles. Leaves the person conscious but immobile for about twenty minutes."

Karoulis knew that there was no decision yet on their legality. "Sixty thousand volts. Christ. Isn't that a lot?"

"The current generated is only point two or three or five milliamps, or something like that. It's slightly misleading, as I understand it."

Karoulis was studying it in his hand when the explosion shattered all the windows around them and blew them over the desk.

Seconds of silence followed, while smoke billowed and curled through the room. Then there were coughs, curses, a couple of shouts, as plaster and glass began to shudder loose from weakened moorings.

Karoulis lay on the floor, half on top of Huziak. It came to him slowly what had happened. At least, he thought, I'm alive. But he hurt everywhere he tried to move. Then his eyes began to sting.

Blood, he thought. And he could taste it in his mouth.

Huziak coughed. Then: "Christ."

Karoulis rolled off the sergeant, onto his side, lay there with his heart pounding. Part of his hearing seemed to be gone. Everything was ringing. With a concerted effort, he focused on Huziak. The sergeant's face was covered in blood.

Jesus, he thought. *Jesus Christ.*

Karoulis and Huziak sat in chairs, watching the team of officers and plainclothesmen sift through the rubble. Karoulis smoked a cigarette openly. Nobody said anything to him about it.

All the blood covering both of them had been caused by superficial cuts from the exploding glass. Simply put, it looked worse than it was. Karoulis had bitten his tongue badly when the blast's concussion bowled them over. The cut on Huziak's cheek indicated that he hadn't missed losing an eye by very much.

Two officers had not been so lucky.

Karoulis eyed the body bags, inhaled deeply on his cigarette.

Evans and Lim. In the wrong place at the wrong time. It could have been anybody. It could have been me, he thought. He closed his eyes, imagining the horror of telling their families.

My office, Karoulis thought. It was in my fucking office. It was meant for me. Those poor bastards were just standing by the door, talking. If I hadn't come out with Huziak . . .

There was a man standing in front of him. It was Polonich from the bomb squad. From a vibrator to this, he thought. A full day.

"Semtex, Captain," Polonich said.

"I'm listening." He exhaled a stream of smoke.

"Odorless, orange-colored plastic explosive, almost impossible to detect."

"Where was it?"

"Taped to the bottom of your desk, I'd say right now."

"How'd it get there?"

Polonich shrugged. "That's the million-dollar question. We'll need a list of everyone who was in and out of your office the past few days. Maybe the past few weeks, if that doesn't pan out."

"Is the stuff common? Easy to get?"

Polonich shook his head. "State of the art. Manufactured by the Eastern Bohemian Works, a state-owned arms factory in the Czech Republic. It's the only substance that defies detection by bomb-sniffing dogs, X-ray machines. Government officials and terrorist experts claim Syria and Libya have used it. This is the first domestic use I've heard of. These guys knew what they were doing."

"Under my desk." Karoulis stared at the remains of his office.

"It can be placed in a suitcase and appear as a dense mass on an X-ray machine. It can also be shaped to resemble innocent-looking objects. It also has the advantage of being stable, meaning it does not go off in uncontrolled circumstances."

"Meaning that it went off exactly when someone wanted it to go off."

Polonich nodded. "I'd say so."

Karoulis turned to Huziak. "I'd like to thank you."

From beneath a long bandage over his left eye, Huziak squinted at him.

"I have a new fondness for zappers."

They stared at the body bags on the floor.

3 "The king of England got his annual six percent raise." Paul Helwig, Mitch's eighty-four-year-old father stared at his son as if the money had come out of his own pocket. He swiveled his head from the TV set, which was his constant companion, and held Mitch steadily with his weakening eyes. "His annual salary's now fifteen point two million dollars. Not bad for an old guy with a crown."

Mitch noticed that his father's sweater was buttoned up incorrectly.

"The whole family of inbred imbeciles have now got twenty million dollars a year to polish their crowns with. Wonder they can get 'em on their heads, the way they must be swellin' up." He shook his own head in disdain. "He's nearly as old as I am, for God's sake. Where did I go wrong? Eh? Where?" He continued to shake his head at the imponderable.

"Maybe next time you'll get it right." Mitch smiled at his father.

"Next time. Yeah. Right. Next time. I'll hold my breath."

Mitch sat down in the worn, green, cloth-covered chair in the corner of the apartment opposite to where his father was sitting. It was a chair that had been a fixture in the home in which he had grown up—the home that had been sold only last year. Paul Helwig had lasted less than a year in the house after Mitch's mother had died. Mitch's parents had been married for fifty-two years. His father still didn't know where he was. It had all happened too fast.

Mitch knew how he felt.

"How're you doing?"

The older Helwig gazed at his son. "This is a strange place. I guess it'll take some gettin' used to." He paused. "I know I'm old. But everybody here's old. Makes me feel weird. Don't think it's natural."

"You wanted to come here. You said you'd researched it, that it was the best spot."

"I know. And it is. Still—"

Mitch nodded. He understood.

"A ninety-nine-year-old Japanese guy reached the top of Mount Fuji yesterday. A record. Forty-five hundred meters. Guy used a cane. The other climbers all shouted 'Banzai.' " He gestured with his hand. "Nobody around here's doin' anything like that."

"Where do you get stuff like that?" Mitch asked.

"Where I get everything. Goddamn TV."

Sandy Zwolinski, the talk-show host with the exquisite white hair, blossomed to life on the screen as they sat there. It was ten A.M.

"Guy on *Canada A.M.* this morning confirmed what I always knew. Bald guys are sexy." He smiled under his shiny dome. Mitch smiled too.

"Scientists have found the missing molecular link. It's all tied to overactive male hormones."

"That one's been kicking around for years."

"It's confirmed. Scientists said so."

"Scientists where? Who?" Mitch continued to smile as he felt himself getting drawn in further. His old man could do it to him every time.

"University of Miami. Oil glands in the scalps of guys with pattern baldness. . . . "

"Pattern baldness?"

Paul Helwig stopped for a second, stared, then continued. "They got molecules, called receptors, with fifty to one hundred percent greater capacity for binding the ingredients of testosterone. Receptors catch the hormones as they enter the scalp, convert 'em to testosterone, then pass 'em on to the gene structure in the cell's nucleus."

Mitch knew that he was getting exactly what his father had heard on TV. The old man's mind and short-term memory were as good as ever. As his eyes faded, the world came to him, as it did to so many others, via the Tube.

"Guess the babes around here better look over their shoulders when you come strolling down to dinner."

"Be like shootin' fish in a barrel. Couldn't even give me a good chase anymore. It's ninety percent women here, you know."

"I know. You've told me."

"Most of 'em are Baptists, though. They subsidize the place. Don't know what to make of 'em yet."

"Just don't ask them to dance."

A corner of the old man's mouth finally smiled.

Fellowship Towers it was called. Senior citizens' apartments, right on Yonge Street, north of Bloor, right near the revamped Canadian Tire Store. It *was* a good spot. There was a considerable waiting list—much longer for women than for men, as they tried in vain to balance their numbers. The facts were, simply, that women outlived men.

Paul Helwig, as usual, was the exception.

There was a dining room on the second floor, along with an elaborate, tasteful sitting and social area. His father had opted for the three-meal-a-day plan, freeing him from most shopping and cooking. With his fading eyes and his fading strength, and his lack of familiarity in the kitchen in general, it was a good deal.

Mitch had listened for years about what a loner his father had considered himself to be. Sometimes, when Mitch would phone, his father would ruefully admit that he had been the

first person in three days that he had talked to. In bad weather,
in winter, that had not been unusual.

Sandy Zwolinski, resplendent beneath his full, white hair, was holding forth into his trademark microphone, his piercing blue eyes twinkling with life—the Dean of Daytime TV.

The older Helwig jerked his head in Zwolinski's direction. "Guy's got too much hair." He smiled. "Poor bugger."

Mitch watched the thin profile that was his father, wondering what to tell him, wondering where to start.

Paul Helwig began again. With his eyes riveted on the tube, he said, "News last night said they'd found a guy, a World War One soldier, found him in a glacier." He turned and looked at Mitch. "Guy spent more than a century in a glacier. Can you imagine? Glacier moved down the Italian Alps. They said his uniform was still in good condition. Found a note in his pocket that said: 'In the event of my death, notify my mother, Fifth District, Vienna.' Poor bastard."

Mitch didn't know what to say.

"Hundred and somethin' years in a fuckin' glacier."

"What're they doing with him?" Mitch asked.

"Guy had a tag around his neck. Born in 1874. Didn't release his identity." He swiveled back to Sandy Zwolinski. "They're gonna look for next of kin." He breathed out heavily. "Good luck."

Then he mumbled it again. "Poor bastard," he said.

Zwolinski's got one of them Revivalists on."

"Who?" asked Mitch.

"Revivalists. You know. Those guys. Scientists." His face crinkled. "Blue Limbo. That stuff."

They watched.

"—guest today is Dr. Victor Heywood, a physiologist at the Stanford Medical Center in California. He's going to tell us more about Revival, what it is, what it can do. And maybe," he paused, "he can tell us what it all means. I know I could use a little enlightenment on it all," Zwolinski said with the proper touch of humility.

It was big news lately. Mitch was more than a little curious too. He glanced at his father. The old man's concentration assured him that he was not alone in his interest.

He slouched back, listening.

"Doctor," Sandy Zwolinski said the word slowly, defining its proper parameters, "can we really bring people back from the dead? That is the question, isn't it, in a nutshell?"

"I believe that is the question, Sandy." The doctor was fortyish, personable; he had obviously done the circuit successfully to end up on Zwolinski's show. Information with panache: *Sesame Street* for adults, thought Mitch.

"The answer," said Heywood, "is yes and no."

"Yes and no," repeated Zwolinski, smiling.

The audience chuckled in response to his orchestration.

Heywood smiled too. "Sounds ambiguous, I know. But like most things in life—and death—it is ambiguous, in many ways."

He paused. Zwolinski didn't interrupt him this time. Nobody said anything.

He continued. "When someone dies, if the body, especially the head, is still in good condition—not crushed, mangled, etc.—we can now normally Revive the person for a maximum of four weeks."

"How, Doctor? How can this be done?"

Heywood took his cue. "The dozen major blood vessels carrying blood into and out of the head are attached to a heart-lung machine, which in turn pumps and oxygenates the blood."

Zwolinski, out of his depth, listened intently.

Mitch Helwig was fascinated.

Paul Helwig, at eighty-four, had his own reasons for wanting to hear every word.

"Artificial kidneys are used to remove metabolic wastes. The liver is replaced by glass columns filled with absorbent

chemicals to remove poisonous elements. Nutrients are also
added to the blood, in addition to substances that balance the
blood's acidity. Brain fluid is also maintained. An electrode, a
tiny chip, is implanted in the skull, where the bone resists electrical interference from muscles; this chip is outside the dura,
the tough membrane that surrounds the brain. It can send signals from the cochlea to a computer for analysis, synthesis and
translation, which can then, in turn, be received by someone
operating the computer. In this way, communication is possible." He paused. "People can now communicate with the dead."

The last sentence was followed by several seconds of ab-
solute silence. The idea dwarfed the words.

"But are they dead? Isn't that the question?" asked Zwolinski finally.

"That's certainly one of the questions. It would appear,
now, to be more a matter of definition than ever."

"You mean, how are we to define 'death'?"

"Exactly. Do we now mean the first time one dies? Or the
second—and so far, final—time one dies?"

"Sounds like a combination of science fiction and voodoo
mumbo-jumbo."

Heywood smiled. "In a way, it does. But," he added, "electrical signals produced in the visual cortex of the brain and
picked up underneath the skull have been used since the late
1980s to drive word-processing software, or a speech proces-
sor. It was one of the methods used to treat amyotrophic lat-
eral sclerosis—ALS, or Lou Gehrig's disease—a degenerative
disease which affects the nerve connections in the cortex. Used
quite successfully, too, I should add. And," he plowed on, realizing that much of his information was too technical, searching for touchstones that would make it seem less incredible,
"little known to most of us, a patent was applied for and
received by a St. Louis lawyer way back in 1988, describing a
machine that could keep a severed head alive. Most of the
equipment necessary for all of this has existed for fifteen or
twenty years. We've just finally put it all together."

"Scientific synthesis, piercing the ultimate barrier."

Heywood smiled. "If you like. Grandiosely phrased, but not essentially incorrect."

"Are there not," asked Zwolinski, leading his guest, "a couple of steps toward death, in medical terms?"

"In both medical terms and in legal terms, up till now there appeared to be two stages. A person could be brain-dead without being legally dead. The body had to die as well. But the area of the brain-dead, the realm of the comatose, has always been a gray area. None of this has been clear. As long as the body could hold together without deterioration, hope always existed. We've tapped into that."

"By hope always existing, you mean—"

"I mean that there have always been cases of someone drowning—especially with children—where they may be submerged at the bottom of a pool or something for fifteen or twenty minutes, and for all intents and purposes are dead. But we have the occasional miraculous revival. In 1989, in a small town in Ontario, Canada, a seventy-nine-year-old man, who had been diagnosed as brain-dead ten weeks earlier, was taken off life-support systems and given the last rites of the Catholic church. His two-year-old grandson shouted 'Grandpa!', and the man sat up in bed and stretched out his arms to the boy. A month later, he bought a new car and was driving around visiting family members. It's all documented at Ottawa Civic Hospital. The man's doctors have no medical explanation for his recovery. Brain scans showed no activity after he'd had heart surgery, leading to the conclusion that he'd suffered irreparable brain damage."

"And cryogenics?" asked Zwolinski.

"Cryogenics assumes the same basic sense of boundless optimism: that as long as the body can be kept in good shape, perhaps someday the mind can be revived. We've been waiting for years for science to catch up to Death. Well, we're getting there."

Mitch watched his father. He had not moved.

The TV faded to a commercial.

"Tell all that," his father said finally, "to the guy in the glacier."

Why only four weeks?" Sandy Zwolinski asked.

Heywood shrugged. "Not sure about that yet. It's something like heart transplants used to be—a form of rejection sets in. We're working on it."

"And there've been how many done?"

"Up to last week, over six hundred in the United States, Canada, and Mexico. Free trade." He smiled. "Europe is beginning to equip its hospitals. Australia too. It'll spread rapidly."

"Why, though, Doctor?" Zwolinski leaned forward so that the camera could capture his earnestness. *"Why* would we really want to do this thing?" He spread his hands elaborately. "What's the point?"

Again, the man from Stanford, California, shrugged. "There are as many reasons as there are people, Sandy. The extra four weeks can be used to finalize personal relationships the way most of us would like them to be finalized. Business can be more effectively transferred. Both the military and the police forces have expressed considerable interest. The ability to Revive—albeit temporarily—a person who has suffered a violent or criminal death, to have them explain how they were killed, who killed them . . . well, you can see for yourself where all this could lead."

"I'm not sure you're right, Doctor. I'm not sure we can see where it will all lead."

"It leads right into the future, Sandy. We're all headed there, whether we want it or not."

The camera shifted from Zwolinski, to Heywood, then back to the celebrity host. The audience watched silently. Then: "Tell us about the subjective effect reported by the subjects themselves," said Zwolinski. "The one the media has picked up on. The color."

He waited. They all waited.

Heywood smiled. "Yes," he said. "That is interesting. All the senses seem to disappear. The mind works, and memory exists. The only sense that seems to operate even partially is something that tricks the optical path to the brain. Those Revived report, consistently, to a person, that they see a world of Blue, nothing but Blue. They describe it as an endless void, an ethereal space." He shrugged again.

"Blue Limbo," said Zwolinski.

Blue Limbo, thought Mitch Helwig, watching in Fellowship Towers. It's the twenty-first century, and we've got Blue Limbo. He looked at his father, thought about Elaine, Barbie, Mario, Karoulis, and everything that had happened, everything that would happen.

"Tell it," Paul Helwig said again, "to the guy in the glacier."

Why aren't you at work?" The old man clicked the TV into silence with the remote.

Now it was Mitch's turn to pause. "I've been sent home. Things are changing. My status is up in the air."

His father waited for more. When it didn't come, he asked, "You still getting paid?"

"For now."

"You in trouble?"

Mitch shrugged. In spite of being almost forty years old, he was beginning to feel like a kid. "There are a lot of questions to answer downtown. The warehouse explosion. Last fall."

Paul Helwig nodded.

"I was involved. I spoiled a lot of parties. It cost powerful people a lot of money."

His father continued staring at him for a while, then put his hand to his chin and stared at the dormant TV set. "I heard," he said, "that every sort of filth was going on in that place, that

its demise was a blessing to civilization." He glanced at Mitch.
"That true?"

"Yes."

"Then," he said, "piss on 'em. You did the right thing. Can you hold your head high?"

"Yes."

"Fuck 'em, then. They want to play their little political games, you step aside. There's more to life than a lunch pail and a job, if you can't hold your head up."

Mitch rose up out of the chair, put his hands in his pockets, and walked to the window nine floors above Yonge Street. He stared down in silence.

Then the old man asked him, "Why don't you go home?"

Mitch turned and stared at him.

The answer was too long in coming. Mitch knew that even through half-blind eyes, Paul Helwig could see the truth etched on his son's face, for he saw his father sag visibly.

Dreams are woven on looms of illusion. There's no other way.

How a dream dies can be impossible to chart. The dream that had been Mitch Helwig's marriage had been unraveling for longer than he had understood, longer than he cared to admit.

It was still dying, scuttled in canyons of memory, in fragments of broken routines.

But he remembered the turning point. He remembered when he finally understood what was happening.

Barbie had just turned nine. Mitch had traded his evening shift with Evans in order to be at home for her birthday party. *Nine years old*, he thought, *and we're still living in an apartment.* They would never, he knew, own their own home. That was another dream that had died, many years earlier, another impossibility that they had slowly let go. For them—Elaine and him—life had become constant compromise, and the truth was that in this they were no different than anyone else in their apartment complex. No different than most others any-where.

But Mitch had only seen the tip of the iceberg gliding in the calm seas before him.

Can Lottie sleep here, Daddy?"

"We promised her mother she'd be home by nine. It *is* a school night."

Barbie had felt the urge to try just one more time. Lottie Patel was, after all, her best friend.

It was 8:30. Mitch was watching the two of them with amusement and something akin to nostalgia—something more like wonder, tinged with deep pleasure. It was one of the re-warding moments of parenthood, these glimpses into inno-cence: to live in a world where candles on a cake can light the world with magic.

He had read *The Catcher in the Rye* in high school—be-cause he had had to—in what seemed to him now like a com-pletely different life. He remembered Holden Caulfield watching his little sister, Phoebe, going round and round on the carousel, remembered how Holden had cried while he watched her. He remembered his English teacher trying to get the class to understand the incident, and how they had shrugged it off.

He understood it now.

Like so many other things.

The V-phone beeped beside him.

Elaine came in from the kitchen as he picked it up.

"Hello."

The video portion remained blank. Then the line went dead.

Mitch caught Elaine staring at him, clutching a handful of birthday napkins. Then she dropped her eyes and went back into the kitchen.

"Daddy?"

Turning his gaze to Barbie, he hung up the cool plastic receiver. He smiled at her. "It must've been a wrong number."

In the kitchen, a drawer shut heavily.

Outside his apartment door, in the hallway, Mitch looked down at Barbie and Lottie, scarcely seeing them. He hadn't moved from where he stood. They both looked up at him expectantly.

"You two run down and press the button for the elevator. I'll be along in a minute." He forced a smile.

"Okay."

He pretended to be checking for keys in his pocket. The girls scurried down the threadbare carpeting of the hallway in a swirl of woolen coats and ponytails, vying for the thrill of pressing the button first.

Muted, but still audible through the door, he heard the beep as Elaine activated the V-phone. Then he heard her muffled voice—the actual words undistinguishable—as she spoke to the person on the other end.

He stood for a few seconds longer, frozen in place, his mind numb. Bits of information, previously disparate, clattered in his head like ice cubes dropped onto a tile floor.

Down the hall, the elevator chimed its arrival. The kids turned to look at him puzzled.

"Dad!"

He hesitated.

The voice, insistent on the far side of the door, the children, waiting for him at the elevator, pulled him in different directions, stretching him until he felt faint.

Nine years old, he thought.

He could hardly breathe.

Then, slowly, moving his feet forward, with a conscious, light-headed motion, he walked toward the children.

*　　*　　*

Mitch swung his feet over the side of the bed and sat up. Elaine stirred beside him. Wearing only his undershorts, the cool air of the apartment at night gave him goose bumps.

He stood up.

Barbie was asleep. Lottie was safely home, tucked into her own bed. He glanced back down at the inert form of his wife.

It was 1:40 A.M. The birthday party was over.

His daughter was nine.

Pulling on his robe, he shut the bedroom door behind him, listening to its soft click. From the hall closet, where it was stored in its obsolescence, he took down the small, cheap cassette recorder that no one used anymore, along with one of the blank cassettes beside it. On his way to the living room, he popped the cassette into the recorder and unfurled the extension cord.

Sitting down on the sofa, he plugged it in and set it beside the V-phone.

He lifted the plastic receiver from its cradle, gripping it with unnecessary pressure, breathing deeply and steadily. Making sure it was off video, he flicked the switch from Tone to Pulse. Then he pressed the Redial button, placed the receiver by the recorder's microphone, and activated the Record button.

The last number dialed was activated. It clicked its memorized ticks into the cassette turning lazily beside it.

For Mitch, they were as loud as thunderclaps.

It rang twice before being answered by a groggy male voice.

"Hello?"

Mitch went cold.

"Hello?"

As if in a dream, Mitch softly hung up the phone, switched off the recorder, unplugged it, and carried it back to its resting place on the top shelf of the hall closet. As he stored it there, he popped the cassette out and dropped it into the pocket of his robe.

Then he went back and sat down on the sofa in the living room. He sat there for half an hour, in the dark, in the silence, his face a mask. The cold of the apartment made him shiver finally, and fighting an impulse that made no sense to him, an impulse to kneel on the floor for no reason that he could think of, he drifted back to bed, careful to stay on his own side, and pulled the covers up to his neck.

He had still been shivering when the alarm went off to tell him that he had to go to work.

And now, standing in his father's apartment, the memories draining away, like raindrops sluicing off oilskin, Mitch focused on the question: *Why don't you go home?*

"Elaine and I aren't living together right now."

Paul Helwig could make no response.

"I've moved out. At least for now."

Still nothing.

"It's been about a month now. I've got a small place—top floor of a house in the Queen and Pape area."

"Barbie?" The word was a mumble, a confused invocation.

Mitch dropped his eyes. "She's with her mother. For now." He paused. "We'll work it out."

"Why didn't you tell me? Why didn't you come to me?"

Mitch shrugged, still unable to meet his father's eyes. "Couldn't." The word hung between them.

His father nodded. Mitch felt like a toddler with a scraped knee.

"Do you need anything? Money?"

Mitch shook his head.

But it was not true. He needed a lot. And he felt helpless.

4 Mitch felt a sense of relief as he drove south on Yonge Street after leaving his father. He had stayed for lunch at noon in the second-floor dining room with him, fascinated by the array of senior citizens around them, the number of people with walkers and wheelchairs. Everyone who went by the table had stopped and spoken to them. In a way, his visit to his father was a visit to all of them as well, and they all savored as much of it as they could.

His father was right. It was strange.

He had enjoyed the lunch. He was with survivors. These were people who had made a peace with life and what it had dealt them. They had come to terms with their own flaws, their bodies, their families. Life could make you crazy, Mitch knew. You had to hang on.

He was trying to hang on.

It was 1:30 P.M. Mitch took in the street scene of joggers in luminescent suits, wired to their Walkmans; a swarm of Asian kids with safety helmets and their new striped roller blades were legging it out in the inside lane a few car lengths ahead of him; and when he crossed Bloor Street, he drove slowly past a group of black and white kids, between the ages of twelve and fifteen, their heads shaved up one side, the steel toes of their boots glinting in the afternoon sun, idling under the Uptown marquee, waiting for the theater to open for the first showing of the latest splatterpunk film in town.

He could never figure why they weren't in school. How

did their parents stand them? Could it happen to him? He
thought of Barbie and weakened at the image.

He had to see her again. Soon.

Mitch eased his aging Chev to the curb on Queen East at
Broadview. The 7-Eleven store had an automatic teller inside,
and he needed some cash. His father had been good, he
thought as he sat behind the wheel, thumbing through his
wallet for a quick inventory. The old man never passed judgment, Mitch realized. At least, he never had on Mitch. He certainly had opinions about everything else. Looking up and
through the windshield at nothing, the power of the bond that
had been forged silently between him and his father hit him
suddenly.

They were both alone. They were both disenfranchised
from the mainstream.

There was nothing left except their children.

Every man became his own father, every woman her own
mother, to varying degrees. He understood that. It was the
speed with which it had happened to Mitch Helwig that surprised him. That, and the clarity of his life that it produced,
made him sit where he was for an extra minute.

A bit of commotion at the end of that extra minute caused
him to refocus on the external world with equal clarity.

It was the middle of the afternoon. The woman getting
into the cab some twenty meters ahead of him was Chinese and
matronly. Her purse hung on a long leather strap over her left
shoulder. Mitch watched without knowing what he was seeing
until it was happening.

Two youths, a Chinese male about seventeen and a blond
Caucasian who seemed slightly younger, appeared from the
7-Eleven behind the woman. In a movement that was both
precise and deft, betraying much practice, almost elegant in its
smoothness, the Chinese boy cut the shoulder strap of the

woman's purse as she leaned forward into the cab and tossed it to the other boy. It had all transpired in a second. Then the two youths sped around the corner on foot, running south on Broadview.

The woman stood stunned.

Mitch felt adrenaline begin to pump. They had probably watched the woman withdraw cash inside the store, knew exactly what they were doing, had done it many times before in many places.

The engine was still idling. But it was more than instinct or training that made Mitch pull out into the traffic and go around the cab and the shocked woman, make a right at the corner and sight the two miscreants running ahead of him. It stemmed from a quiet outrage against all that had happened to him and all that was still going to happen. Instead of making his brain blur, it calmed it into a cold steel.

He thought of his father. The woman getting into the cab would lose enough in life. She didn't need to lose this as well.

He felt under the seat beneath him to make sure it was still there.

The sun-face painted high on the side of the gaudy Caribbean restaurant smiled down on him as he watched the two snatchers run past the chain-link fence on his right and head west up the alley beside the five-storied redbrick factory. Mitch pulled up to the mouth of the alley, gazing down its length through the passenger window. There was another chain-link fence at the far west side, with the plastic pennants of a used-car lot fluttering aloft above it. They turned left, heading south, out of his line of vision, behind the factory.

Mitch cruised slowly down Broadview, along the front of the factory, to the lane which bordered the south side of the building. The lane ran around the factory in a squared-off U, surrounded by wire fence on all sides. Directly in front of him, along the south border, the entrance ramp for the Eastern Avenue expressway across the Don River isolated the spot even more.

The youths had not reappeared here. They were at the back of the building, or they were inside. There was no place else they could be.

Mitch looked at the signs on the structure: GATEWAY AUTO COLLISION, DUBOIS MARINE INSURANCE, M. CUTRARA & SON, WHOLESALE FRESH PRODUCE. And in spite of the blue, diamond-shaped sign that read FOR LEASE, there was definitely business transpiring inside. It certainly was not abandoned.

They were at the back, then.

The Chev moved slowly down the north alley. Ahead of him, the red-and-white plastic pennants, time-worn and weathered, fluttered at the edge of the wire fence, announcing rows of gray, assembly-line Toyotas, the dust from the nearby expressway covering them like urban delta silt.

Mitch made a left, along the building's rear.

They were there.

Turning, they watched him come, defiantly.

On an abandoned loading platform, the two youths had dumped the purse's contents, spreading it out: wallet, coins, credit cards, a few bills, comb, small makeup kit. Their arrangement of the contents was in itself an affront.

Mitch pulled up about ten meters away, staring at them through his opened driver's side window. He let the car idle for fifteen seconds before shutting it off, while the two youthful felons studied him silently.

Approaching age forty, Mitch thought, gave a man many second thoughts. One of them was the uncertainty regarding just what one was and was not still capable of doing physically. As he eyed the two young and seemingly fit males, this thought did flit across his mind.

He reached under the seat and extracted the bag that he

kept stored there. Clutching it in his hand, he opened the door and stepped out.

The two thieves straightened, unblinking.

Mitch reached into the bag and pulled out the Barking Dog. It had been a while since he had used it. In fact, he remembered having sworn to try to avoid using it. But then, he thought, these things happen.

Their eyes narrowed as they watched him attach it. They knew what it was: the ultimate in modern lie detection technology. Not even the police were supposed to have it, and they knew this too.

Who was this guy?

Mitch Helwig snapped the pocket-sized silver trinket to his belt where it could gaze unhindered at the faces before him. He then attached the sticky electrode to the bare flesh of his rib cage under his shirt.

The two young jackals watched him.

"What's that?" The blond Caucasian spoke first.

The Chinese lad turned a disdainful gaze on him for breaking the silence in any way.

Mitch smiled. The smile was cold. "Easter Bunny left it." He focused the eye. The Dog's microcomputer would cross-reference voice pitch, body odors, face temperature, pupil and retina response; the microwave respiration monitor would measure stomach palpitations caused by rapid breathing under stress; and the video input would scan for the spontaneous, subcortical facial expressions that could register with the machine's coding system.

If either of these two told even the slightest lie, the Barking Dog would howl by sending a jolt of icy sensation to Mitch's side, where the electrode clung to his flesh.

The Oriental picked up a knife from the loading platform behind them—the same knife, Mitch assumed, that had originally severed the purse's shoulder strap. The sun glinted hotly from its surface. Mitch also noted the look in their eyes: like distant thunder.

Then he noticed something else about the two. The hand that held the knife also flashed in the sun, its metal fingers twisting the light. The blond lad sidled a meter or so to the left of his cohort, his silver foot creating the slightest trace of a limp as it sparkled lightning from the rubble around it.

Bionic limbs, Mitch realized.

These two were well on their ways to whatever technological future awaited them. Piece by piece, they were ceding their humanity, tying motor and sensory nerve impulses to an electronic, computerized control system.

Mitch was struck by the irony of the confrontation. The human-machine interface was all about them. The Barking Dog. The limbs. Even the automatic teller that had complied with the Chinese woman's electronic commands. And it was just the beginning.

The Chinese boy apparently had been thinking. "If you're a cop," he said, "then you'd better read us our rights. If not," the silver hand clutching the knife remained poised aloft in the sunlight, "then you'd better fuck off."

Nobody moved.

Mitch could not tear his eyes from the hand, the foot. Individual nerve fibers, axons, regenerated through holes mere microns in diameter, like string beans growing through chicken wire, he thought. Commercial plasma-etching technology. Iridium microelectrodes, coated with silicon nitride to protect them from degradation caused by bodily fluids.

One day cops, he had been told at a criminology seminar, might be able to plug their nerve impulses directly into their skimmer's control system.

Silicon nitride versus bodily fluids.

He thought of Elaine, Barbie, Karoulis, Mario, his father. He thought of Blue Limbo and the light-speed at which they were all approaching it.

The planet seemed to tilt, sliding the two steel-enhanced creatures dangerously near to him. He observed them with a brilliant clarity, suffused by the surrounding heat and cinders.

Mitch licked his lips. "You stole that purse." The Barking Dog waited, infinitely patient.

The Chinese youth stepped forward. He tried to assess Mitch Helwig, the Barking Dog. Mitch saw the knife more clearly now—a simple Arkansas toothpick, polished carbon steel, twenty-four centimeters overall. The other boy took a Ni baton from his belt, pressed the release bar and automatically extended it from its closed twenty centimeters to its fully extended fifty-two centimeters. Mitch knew all about them. The Taiwan Provincial Police still used them. Steel tubing, light. Capable of delivering stunningly painful blows.

"You made a mistake coming here," the blond one said.

Where did creatures like this come from? Mitch wondered. From under what rock? And we patch them up with new and better limbs, so they can continue. He remembered the story of the so-called Crocodile Man in the recent news, the name the health experts had given to a particularly brutal punk who had been apprehended while dismembering his latest victim. They said the "crocodile" brain condition was brought on by the assailant's having been born with the umbilical cord wrapped around his neck. The Crocodile Man, so went the contention, operated hyperactively, unhindered by functions of that portion of the brain governing emotions, morals, or the ability to judge reality.

Moral imbeciles. Egocentric instead of ecocentric. How many of them were out there? What else caused that portion of their brains to cease functioning?

"You stole that purse," Mitch repeated.

"We found it," said the blond boy. His silver foot ground into the cinders as he shifted his weight.

The cold of blatant fabrication froze Mitch's side. It began to freeze Mitch in other ways too. He could feel his anger rising and tried to control it.

Fuckers, he thought.

They began to move apart from one another, leaving the

purse forgotten between them, never turning from the still figure of the man confronting them.

Mitch immobilized them again. "Are you two a pair of morons? You think I'd just waltz in here and submit to a pair of assholes like you?"

They stared without comprehension. The sun was at the stranger's back, making them squint, outlining him incandescently.

"I guess you figure you're a pair of real bad guys. Tough guys. Guys who'd kill for nickels and dimes." Mitch was taunting them, waiting to hear their voices.

"We never killed nobody," said the blond boy.

But it was a lie. The Barking Dog told Mitch Helwig so.

The Chinese boy glanced at his cohort. He was sharp enough to at least determine that the stranger now knew something more about them than that they were a couple of minor purse snatchers. What he didn't know was what this man would do about it. The guy wasn't following any of the patterns that they'd seen before, and this new scenario wasn't computing smoothly in his jangled synapses. The Barking Dog wasn't any legal threat. Its data was inadmissible. The courts hadn't figured out what to do with it yet.

So what was this all about?

It was about Mitch Helwig's anger, his frustration. He felt it bubbling to the surface, beginning to smoke silently.

They began to move toward him. As they did so, he reached once again into the bag from which he had taken the Barking Dog. He aimed the small laser that he pulled out in their general direction.

They stopped.

"The bag of goodies is surprising, isn't it?"

They said nothing. The lightweight plastic Sanyo could burn a hole in them as neat as a pin.

Mitch gestured casually toward them with the laser. "Put those things down and relax."

"Suppose we don't," said the older one.

Mitch shrugged. "You only look stupid, is what I figured." He waited. "Maybe I was wrong. Maybe I'll have to kill you." He straightened his arm, targeting.

They lowered their weapons to the ground.

"You two little pigs stole that lady's money. I watched you. Then you ran like little pigs back here to your pigpen to play with it. And now," he took a breath, "you tell me that you're killers."

"We never told you nothin'."

Mitch eyed them steadily. "You boys are all confused. You're all mixed up."

The staring contest continued.

"Consider me your new social worker."

The darker, older boy tried one last bit of bravado. "Don't mess with us. You don't know what you're messin' with."

Mitch smiled slowly, chillingly. "Lines from old, bad videos. It's your stock in trade, all you know." He stepped closer to them. He was no longer a cop. He was no longer even Mitch Helwig. He didn't know what he was or how this had happened to him, but it happened more and more often of late. His job as cop was so limited, his desire to make a difference overwhelming. Maybe he was going crazy. In fact, he knew that it was partly true. It was as he had thought while driving from Fellowship Towers on Yonge Street: the world could make you crazy; it was making him crazy. There seemed to be no end to it all.

"As your new social worker," he said, "I think we'll start with basic Pavlovian conditioning. You do something mean to somebody else, you break the law, and you pay."

"What about if you break the law?" The question came from the Oriental boy and hung in the air like a storm warning.

A cloud of memories, of dark perceptions, billowed up behind Mitch Helwig's eyes. "I pay," he said. The swirl of knowledge eddied away. "Everybody pays."

There was a sheen of sweat on the blond boy's brow now. The hot afternoon sun was a very small part of it.

"You pay me. I'm the reason you're going to try real hard to behave from now on."

They waited.

"First lesson," Mitch said. "Empty your pockets. Now."

Coins, billfolds, pocket combs tumbled out. Each of them had one more weapon as well—the blond, a Black Stallion knife, with solid brass liners and buffalo horn handle; the Chinese lad dropped a more conventional folding trench knife with built-in knuckle duster.

"Over there." Mitch gestured to the fence with a wave of the laser. They made their way across the cinders, the blond's silver foot an eerie, alternating glint. "Now," he added, "you, flashfoot, over there." He motioned to a spot some ten meters away.

The boy obeyed.

"Both of you," Mitch said, "lie face down."

"You could kill us," blurted the younger one.

"I could kill you now, as you stand there." Mitch held the laser steady. "A sweep of this across the area would cut you both in half." He paused. "Any doubts?"

They both knelt down, then spread themselves forward on their stomachs.

"Maybe this is what your victims always feel like," Mitch added.

Glancing over at their sprawled forms, an image of the walkers and wheelchairs that he had seen at lunch surfaced, superimposing itself on the reality of the bionic limbs in front of him. The stark injustice, the skewing of balance was not lost on him.

Leaving them there for a moment, Mitch went over to their pocket contents and picked up their billfolds. Briefly, he flipped each open to assure himself that there was some form of ID inside, then popped them into his own pocket.

It was in this moment of inattention that it happened. The Chinese lad must have had it inside his sleeve, and Mitch Helwig later chastised himself for his uncustomary lack of thoroughness, his distracted focus. It took a slice of skin a half centimeter thick from his left shoulder as it passed by, finally thumping numbingly into the wooden door atop the loading platform.

The pain, he knew, would follow in seconds. By all rights, he should be dead by now.

The hilt of the ballistic knife remained in the youth's hand. Good to a range of about ten meters, the weapon was capable of being fired silently and accurately; the penetration was more than five times that of a forceful manual stab. In close quarters, it was merely a knife. He'd seen them for sale on Yonge Street for fifty-nine dollars.

With the onset of pain, he felt the warm trickle of blood down both his back and chest.

Mitch moved quickly toward the prone figure, the sudden pain alerting his primal instincts. The youth lay frozen, fear in his eyes, with the knowledge a big-game hunter might have after a failed shot had turned a rhino in his direction. Mitch kicked him full in the face, swiveling in one fluid motion to face the blond, the Sanyo quivering in his tensed fist, his mind trying to regain total control. He bit down hard on the pain and anger, the laser trained like a cobra on the remaining youth.

"Don't," the boy said.

Mitch remained silent, his glare like ice.

"Don't kill me."

A wave of pain from his shoulder unsteadied him momentarily. The blood from the wound began to flow past the Barking Dog's electrode, gathering at his beltline. In his eyes, Mitch felt the sting of saltwater, uncertain whether it was sweat or tears.

The Chinese youth was unconscious at his feet, his nose and mouth bleeding. Alternately glancing between his two prisoners, Mitch Helwig came to a decision. The bionic hand

of the boy at his feet—the hand that had missed taking Mitch
Helwig's life by centimeters—lay sprawled open like some
metal spider creeping from its black sleeve.

He bent to pull the sleeve back, exposing the silver forearm.

The other boy watched with wide eyes.

Training the Sanyo at the middle of the steel forearm,
Mitch cut the hand off.

Even in the stupor of unconsciousness, the youth's feet
jerked spasmodically. Bionic limbs, unlike simpler prosthetics,
sensed heat and cold.

And pain.

Mitch kicked the hand away dramatically. Then he turned
toward the blond boy and, gritting his teeth at his own pain,
focused the laser on the boy's foot.

"Don't." The boy was terrified now, his eyes wild.

"You guys should think about this," Mitch said. "What it
feels like." He continued to aim the Sanyo.

"Please."

Mitch was shaking now, a combination of rage, fear, and
massive jolts of adrenaline. The blood loss was increasing too,
making him light-headed, mistrusting his own anger. He tried
to steady his hand.

"Please."

Mitch walked slowly toward the prone boy. "You shouldn't
hurt people. You should leave people alone who don't bother
you, who don't deserve to be treated the way you treat them."

The boy had a real, deep fear etched on his face. His
voice quavered. "I'll try," he said.

Mitch halted as the Barking Dog registered the statement. There was a drop of cold attached to the phrase, but
there was also the tremor, the shiver of uncertainty.

There was hope, even if it was born of fear.

Mitch lowered his laser. He stared at the metallic foot.
Then he met the young man's eyes. "You'll never know," he
said, "how close you came."

The boy was crying now.

Mitch left him there. He gathered up the contents of the lady's purse and refilled it. Then, returning to the unconscious Oriental's form, he bent over and picked up the silver hand and attached half-triceps. Sliding behind the wheel of his Chev, he tossed his own weapon and utility pouch, along with everything else, into the backseat.

Touching his right hand to the searing pain of his left shoulder, he tore the shirt away, baring the wound, twisting his neck for a glimpse. Blood was all he could see.

Starting the engine, he stared through his own tears at the crying blond boy.

5 Besides hurting all over, Phil Huziak was scared. Even though he had put in twenty-two years as a cop, he had never before suffered any form of assault. In fact, he had only drawn his gun twice. The second time— to force a suspect from a car—had shaken him up so badly that he had set his sights on getting off the streets and into an office job with a concentrated determination.

That had been twelve years ago. The job of staff sergeant, which he had held since then, suited him perfectly, and he had no higher aspirations. He liked organizing the reports, setting the schedules. He liked being efficient. He prided himself on oiling all the gears that needed attention, on keeping tabs on the week's procedures.

Let's face it, he thought. I'm a desk man. And glancing down at the bulk of stomach above his belt showed him just how well he had come to fill the mold.

But this shit, he thought. Karoulis and Helwig. Fucking bomb blasts. Evans and Lim. How, he thought, did I get into this?

The hospital had sent him home. He would certainly live. And now, sitting in his own living room, waiting for Norma to come home from work, he found that he was afraid.

I could have died, he thought. I could be Evans or Lim. This is nuts. This morning they were alive, laughing, joking.

What had Karoulis and Helwig brought on him? What had they brought on them all?

*　　*　　*

The phone beeped and he looked at it. Norma, he thought.

"Hello?"

"Phil Huziak, please?"

"Speaking."

"Phil, it's Joseph Galecki."

Huziak was mildly surprised. "Sir," he said. He flicked on the video, and the face of the deputy chief appeared.

"I'm calling to make sure everything's okay, Phil. Is there anything I can do?"

Huziak sighed, not knowing what to say. "I guess I'm okay. Shaken up, though."

"Of course you're shaken up. I can't tell you how glad I am that that's the extent of it for you. It is, isn't it?"

"Seems to be, sir."

"Sam Karoulis isn't with you, is he?"

"No, sir. He isn't."

"He hasn't gone home yet. I called. You know where he is?"

"I haven't seen him since the hospital."

"Hmm." Galecki's face became pensive.

"Anything I can do for you, sir?"

Galecki seemed to be thinking. "We should be doing things for you, Phil. But these are the kinds of crises that test us." It was Galecki's turn to sigh. "Can I ask you to do something for me, Phil?"

Huziak had a bad feeling. "I guess so."

"It's really Karoulis's job. But since I can't find him, and we can't let this go on much longer . . . "

Huziak's heart sank.

"Somebody has to tell Evans and Lim's families. And I don't think it should come from some cop on a motorcycle or in a black-and-white."

"I understand."

"I'd do it myself, but I've got the chief of police, the
mayor, and three TV crews waiting outside for me."

And what's more important? thought Huziak. "I understand."

"You're okay with it, Phil?"

"No problem, sir."

"Thanks a million. I owe you. Take care."

"Don't worry about it."

The screen went blank.

Don't worry about it. Why should he worry about it?
Huziak began to simmer. He hasn't just been blown around a
room by a bang that still has his ears ringing. And now he
doesn't have to face the families. I do. Good old Huziak. *Me*.

Fuck, he thought. Fuck me.

Joseph Galecki rubbed his forehead with his right hand, trac-
ing his fingers along the hairline as he tried to tie together the
day's loose ends in his mind. Helwig. Karoulis. Huziak. Evans.
Lim.

Helwig.

It started and ended with him. As before.

And he would have to try to find answers for everybody.
They would expect it of him.

He ran a pocket comb through his tinted hair, formu-
lating what he would say to the press, waiting like hounds
outside his door. Then he arose and went to meet them, ap-
propriating the correct, precise facial expression for a moment
before stepping out into the hall.

6 Mitch closed the door of his third-floor apartment behind him and leaned against the wall. His shoulder, bleeding freely, needed to be treated. Having lived there for only one month, there wasn't much in the place that he could think of using to stem its flow. His medicine cabinet didn't even have a bottle of aspirin in it yet.

He began unbuttoning his shirt, pulling it from his belt. The pain was intense and accelerated sharply whenever he made any movement that affected the shoulder. Moving into the kitchen area, he finally shrugged out of the shirt, winced anew, then tossed the blood-soaked garment into the sink. He leaned forward on the edge of the counter, breathing deeply through his mouth, trying to control both his thoughts and the constant throb and sting of the wound.

He gritted his teeth as a new wave of pain stabbed at the open cut. "Shit." The word echoed in the empty apartment.

He threw back his head and bit on his lower lip. Tilting his eyes sideways, he glanced into the living area to his right. The single item of furniture in his range of vision was a wicker chair that he had borrowed from the woman on the second floor.

He had left his previous life behind.

He was alone.

And he wasn't sure that he liked that very much at all.

With his one and only dish towel tied as tightly as he could manage, with one hand, around his shoulder, Mitch began to take stock more rationally. What came next?

He wasn't sure.

He'd live. He knew that. The quality of that life was what he didn't know.

He looked around the place that was now his home. In a previous generation, this had been the attic of the house. He had his own entry up the house's side stairs—a circular, wooden stairway—that ended in the small landing outside the unit's door. It had been advertised in *The Globe and Mail* as a studio apartment, with one bedroom, a den, a galley kitchen and living room combo. It measured all of about fifty square meters, Mitch guessed. Big enough for what he was bringing with him: nothing.

In the center of the apartment where he was standing, it was fine. But as you moved toward the walls, the ceiling sloped and the headroom disappeared. He'd hit his head a number of times, and doing the dishes without stooping was impossible, so the landlady had left him a stool to sit on for that purpose. The bathroom door didn't open all the way because it opened inward and hit the wall sink. But his options had been limited, as had his finances. And he couldn't beat the rent.

His glance strayed into the bedroom. He had been sleeping on a ten-centimeter-thick piece of foam that he had purchased at Sears in Gerrard Square. On it was the sleeping bag that had been his since he was a kid. Not much was going to be able to be transported up that winding stairway.

Except Barbie. She was the only thing from the past that he wanted. And needed.

The sound of the door buzzer startled him. He knew that it was his buzzer because he had tested it and heard it, but this was the first time that anyone else had pressed it. Opening the door, he went out onto the small landing outside his entranceway and opened the window there, peering down into the driveway.

The face of Karoulis, his captain, turned to look up at him.

Inside the apartment, Sam Karoulis and Mitch Helwig stared at each other.

"Jesus," said Karoulis, taking in Mitch's shoulder.

Mitch surveyed the cuts on Karoulis's face. "You need a new blade in your razor, Captain."

Karoulis shook his head, smiled wryly, and looked away. Then he asked, "What happened to you?" His eyes were scanning the apartment.

"What happened to *you?*"

Karoulis looked back at Mitch. "That's what I came here to see you about." He shrugged. "Stuff you should know."

Mitch waited.

Karoulis looked around the apartment again. "I'm sorry, Mitch. I didn't know."

Mitch said nothing.

"I phoned your place to talk to you. Elaine answered. She gave me your phone number. I thought about it a bit, then I called her back and asked for your address. Thought I'd come and see you, see how you're doing."

Mitch shrugged. "So how'm I doing?" He looked around his own apartment. The two men continued to stand opposite one another awkwardly.

"You know Mitch, I've been there."

Mitch frowned.

"Separated. Divorced. I remember this." His hand gestured casually, indicating the apartment.

"I didn't know."

"It was a long time ago." Karoulis was quiet for a moment. "But you don't forget." He studied Mitch's face with a measure of compassion. "You never forget."

Mitch nodded. It rang true. He knew that he would never forget.

"You know," Karoulis said, "in Nebraska, they call someone who saws a man in half a magician." He looked at Mitch. "Here, they call him a divorce lawyer."

Mitch smiled.

Karoulis shrugged. "It's the job," he said. "Destroys you. Destroys your family. Happens more and more." He took out a cigarette. "Mind?"

Mitch shook his head.

Karoulis flicked a lighter and inhaled deeply. He held the smoke in his lungs for a moment, savoring the effect, then exhaled in a steady stream toward the ceiling. Mitch strode into the living area and opened the swivel skylight.

"Nice touch," said Karoulis, walking over under it and motioning upward. He inhaled again, this time blowing the smoke up and through the opening. "I must be the last guy in North America to be doing this. The rest of them have all been hunted down by the Citizens for a Better Everything. I'm a dinosaur." He looked at Mitch. "Maybe you are too."

Mitch nodded. "Maybe I am." He continued to nod without meeting Karoulis's eyes.

"Let's see," said Karoulis, thinking. "When the next chief of police is gone, how'll they word the ad?" He squinted, as if visualizing it. He motioned in the air with his cigarette hand for emphasis. "WANTED: Police chief for multicultural city, population umpteen million. Must administer annual budget of less than a billion dollars and manage enough employees to fill a medium-sized town, including six thousand police officers. Preferred candidate must uphold traditional law enforcement principles, and satisfy public demand for greater accountability." He looked at Mitch. "Pay: one hundred sixty-five thousand dollars a year. Nonnegotiable. That's more than the premier of the province. There's guys who'll line up for that."

Mitch just watched him, silent.

"On the other hand," he continued, "criminals make more

money from the sale of illegal drugs alone than the total interest on the world's debt. Drug dealing is second in annual profits only to armaments and slightly ahead of the oil business." He inhaled more smoke. "And here we stand, all bandaged up. With one fuckin' chair between us. I'm not sure I get it." The smoke streamed out of his mouth and nose as he finished.

Mitch put his hands in his pockets. He wasn't sure that he got it either. He looked over at Karoulis, seeing him differently. "When were you divorced, Captain?"

Karoulis expelled a bit more smoke as he collected his thoughts. "Fourteen years ago." He paused. "I'm fifty-four years old, Mitch." Then he smiled. "And I feel every one of those years." He looked over at Mitch. "You're what? Thirty-eight? Thirty-nine? Forty?"

Mitch just nodded.

"That's when it happened to me. I remembered it all when I talked to Elaine. I remembered what it felt like."

What it felt like, thought Mitch. What it still feels like.

"Keepin' a marriage together today. Two people workin'. All the bullshit around you." Karoulis shrugged helplessly. "I sometimes don't know how the fuck anybody does it. You factor into all that the fact that you're a cop, and, well... I've seen the stats."

Mitch just listened.

"At least fifteen percent of the force has drinking problems. We got a program in place now to try to deal with it. Six out of every ten marriages involving police officers are breaking up. National average is four out of ten. I've seen a couple of studies that indicate divorce is twice as high among police as in other occupations."

Mitch knew that Karoulis was repeating the stats out of kindness, as a sedative. He hung his head and let him continue, understanding the gesture.

"Average life span for a cop here is fifty-seven years,"

Karoulis went on, battling his own self-consciousness. "National average for a male is in the mid-seventies—over eighty for a woman. Every time a cop swallows his gun, the party line is 'he didn't commit suicide because of a police problem; it was a personal problem and had nothing to do with his job.'" He shook his head. "It always has to do with the job, because a cop is a cop. Marital, alcohol, drug abuse, medical, financial— Christ, you name it, we got it. And *how* we got it. We even got an International Law Enforcement Stress Association for Chrissake, and a magazine called *Police Stress.*"

"Maybe the answer to my problem is in the magazine's letter column."

Karoulis arced his cigarette out through the skylight with a flick of his finger. He glanced at the blood-soaked dish towel wrapped around Mitch's shoulder. "Yeah. Right," he said. "So what's that all about?" he asked, indicating the wound. "I send you home, and you take a detour through a shooting range or something?"

But Karoulis had opened the door to his own personal life, and Mitch deflected the conversation back. Seeing Karoulis from this new vantage point gave him a clearer perspective on his own situation—a perspective that he needed badly.

Karoulis knew this. It was why he had come.

"Fifty-seven," Mitch said.

"It's the average," said Karoulis.

"I've never felt particularly average."

Karoulis met his eyes. "Me neither," he said.

So what do you do? Eat standin' up?"

Mitch smiled. "I'm not doing a lot of cooking yet."

"I got a patio table and chairs. Plastic stuff—but good. You can have 'em. Till you get set up properly."

"Okay." Mitch nodded. "Thanks."

"I got a lot of shit you can have, actually. You can clean

out my basement. It'd be a fuckin' blessing. Helen'd write you into her will if you'd do it. She'd write me into her will if *I'd* do it."

Mitch's mind was assimilating Karoulis's offers, while at the same time derailing casually and often through the various domestic corridors that had been cast open between the two men. "When did you marry Helen?" he asked. Somehow, this interested him more than the acquisition of furniture. Even as he asked it, though, he knew that it betrayed some fundamental social lapse, some revealing shift of priorities. I need a table and chairs, he thought suddenly.

Karoulis put his hands in his pockets and frowned up through the skylight. "We've been married ten years," he said.

"And your daughter?" Mitch persisted.

"Maria."

"Maria. You've mentioned her, but I've forgotten."

"She's twenty-five years old. Doing graduate work at McGill. Studying geography."

"So she was eleven when you were divorced."

Karoulis could see what Mitch was thinking. "How old is Barbie?"

Nine, thought Mitch. She's nine years old.

But he couldn't say it out loud.

Your shoulder," Karoulis asked finally to break the silence. "What happened?"

"It was personal."

"Personal, my ass."

"I was doing a little community work with some local teens. I felt that they needed a strong . . . ," he hesitated, " . . . father-figure. They disagreed." He paused. "We worked it out. It's all square now."

"You should see a doctor. Get some stitches."

Mitch looked at his shoulder. It was true. He should see a doctor.

"What the hell am I going to do with you, Helwig?"

Mitch shook his head. "What happened to you, Captain?"

Karoulis produced another cigarette. He got it going before he began. Then he told Mitch Helwig about the zapper, about the Semtex, and about Evans and Lim, while the storm clouds of understanding rolled into Mitch's brain. In a flash of sheet lightning, Mitch glimpsed the larger picture, saw outside the shattered confines of the office being described.

"They wanted me," Mitch said.

Karoulis stared at him, then nodded.

"And," he added, "they wanted you too."

Karoulis blew a cloud of smoke fiercely through the skylight. "No question," he said. "We were to be terminated together."

Mitch went cold.

"You expected otherwise?"

Mitch shrugged. "I don't know."

"I do. These aren't teenagers, and this isn't community work. This is for all the marbles. This is for keeps."

"For keeps," Mitch mumbled. "Everything's for fucking keeps." He walked to the front dormer and looked down at the street below. Two boys were playing road hockey. "Evans and Lim." He felt empty inside. "You spoken to their families?"

"No," he said. His voice had a tinge of shame in it. "I'm sort of AWOL right now."

Mitch closed his eyes. But the sounds of the sticks on the asphalt and the shouts from below only got louder.

7

Huziak sat in his car outside Mike Evans's home. Because he had phoned ahead, he knew that Donna Evans was inside with the two kids.

Good old Huziak. Give him the shit work.

He felt angry. He felt angry at Galecki, angry at the cretin who had placed the bomb, angry at himself for always letting himself get pushed into these things. And he wasn't feeling too kindly towards Helwig or Karoulis either just now. In fact, everyone and everything pissed him off immensely as he sat there simmering.

Evans and Lim were dead. Evans was a guy everybody liked—a good guy, willing to be the butt of the joke. He was twenty-seven years old, a kid from Scarborough who had grown up in the suburbs, a pretty straight shooter. Eddie Lim was thirty-one years old. He had grown up on Gerrard Street, in the Chinese community. He and his wife had a little girl eighteen months old. Huziak had met Lim's father, a man who had done well and worked hard to make the restaurant he owned prosper, and who, when he had met him, was clearly proud of Eddie's acceptance onto the force.

Huziak also remembered the chat he had had with Eddie Lim about a month ago. Ironic now, he thought. Over coffee, they had read an article in the *Sun* about the Blue Limbo machine.

"No way," Eddie had said. "No fuckin' way they'd put me in that thing."

"It depends," Huziak had said.

"On what? What could it depend on?"

Huziak hadn't been able to articulate it. "Just depends."

"On what?" He remembered Eddie grinning. Pearly white teeth. Eyes smiling too.

"Stuff," Huziak had said. "Lots of stuff." He tried to imagine the vast sea of blue nothingness, the zone where you might make amends. He had thought of things he might tell Norma.

"No fuckin' way," Eddie had said, life brimming from him like a wave. Smiling that smile.

Well, Huziak thought, his hands still resting lightly on the bottom of the steering wheel in front of him, don't worry Eddie. You've been spared.

And then Donna Evans came out of the house and stood on the front porch, waiting for him, clearly distressed.

Good old Huziak.

Fuck you, Galecki. Fuck you good for this.

He stepped out of the car.

Donna Evans was wringing her hands.

8 Mitch Helwig had read about black holes in space. A massive star evolves, exhausts its nuclear fuel, then explodes as a supernova. If the star is massive enough, the core will collapse, forming the profound and awesome place where there is nothing.

Mitch felt like he had been there.

After Karoulis had left, his glance fell upon the phone sitting on the floor in the corner of the room, and his memory pulled something else into that great emptiness.

The phone. The tape recorder.

He remembered the day after he had pressed the Redial button for Elaine's last number, approaching Huziak with his tape. Good old Huziak. He'd do what was needed, Mitch knew.

He had placed it beside the Styrofoam coffee cup on Huziak's desk.

The staff sergeant looked at it, looked up at Mitch. "What's that?"

"I need a favor."

"Big or small?"

"Small."

"I'm listening." Huziak sat back in his chair, fingers entwined across his wide stomach.

"There are the pulse clicks from a phone number on the tape. I need it slowed down to pick up the number. Then," he added, "I need a name and an address."

Huziak listened. Whatever he was thinking, he was discreet enough not to say it. He just nodded. "Okay," he said. "I'll send it upstairs. Should have it later today."

Mitch found himself embarrassed within the man's calm radius. "Thanks. I appreciate it." He hesitated a second, uncertain, then turned and left.

The next morning, Huziak had hailed him as he came through the door. "Mitch."

"Sarge."

"I got your package." He handed him a brown, sixteen-by-twenty-four-centimeter envelope. Mitch could feel the tape inside. "They got what you wanted. It's in there."

"Any problems?"

Huziak shook his head slowly. "None."

"I owe you."

"Everybody owes everybody. Big fuckin' deal. Glad to help."

Mitch stuffed it under his arm. With a quick wave of his hand, he was on his way.

Fifteen minutes later, alone in his skimmer, Mitch had torn off the end of the envelope and dumped the contents onto the dashboard in front of him. His fingers flicked away the plastic cassette and picked up the piece of paper underneath it. He amazed himself with the steadiness of his hand as he held it and read what was printed there: *Donald Barbour, Edenbridge Drive, Etobicoke, Ont.*, and a phone number.

Staring vacantly through his windshield, he felt himself suspended in a void. His hand remained the steady fixture that had become his external pose. But inside, rivers of madness pumped wildly through his heart.

Donald Barbour, Mitch thought.

Elaine's boss.

*   *   *

The next day Mitch had visited Guardian Intelligence and Protective Services in Thorncliffe Plaza—the same place where he had bought the Barking Dog and the Silent Guard. He had paid cash for both items.

Cash had a way of imprinting a person on one's memory. Especially the kind of cash that he had paid. He thought that the lanky salesman recognized him.

"Good day, sir."

Mitch Helwig nodded.

The salesman went back to shuffling papers at the counter, letting the customer look about.

Mitch scanned the counters on the opposite side of the store, taking in the eclectic assortment of infrasonics, ultrasonics, and lasers displayed there.

He had seen it all before, but it never failed to both fascinate and repel him. The Phasor Property Guard was aligned beside the Phasor Shock Wave Pistol Series. Below that was an Invisible Pain Field Generator and a kit selling plans for $10.95 that detailed how to construct a 25-Khz, 125-watt ultrasonic oscillator.

"Can I help you with anything?" The salesman forced a modest smile.

Mitch's eyes came back into focus. He had a pretty good idea what he was looking for. He turned to face the man directly. "Listening devices," he said.

"Ah." The salesman turned and brought down a carton from a shelf in back of him. "We have all kinds." Reaching into the carton, he produced a tiny, plain brown box, setting it out before the customer. "Depends on what you're looking for."

Mitch said nothing.

"This one," the salesman said, continuing on in the absence of response, "broadcasts both sides of a telephone conversation to any nearby FM radio. Crystal-clear reception. Exceptional range. Its unique feature is that it only transmits a signal when the telephone is being used, thus conserving the batteries. You can listen in on home or office while performing other duties. Installs simply anywhere on your phone line and doesn't interfere with normal telephone operation."

Mitch was thinking. "How much?"

"The plans are $14.95. The kit is $69.95. An assembled and fully tested unit retails for $99.95."

Mitch nodded. He wasn't sure. "What else you got?"

"Well," the salesman gazed into the box, "there are other items that attach to a phone. But if you're thinking of just listening in on a conversation—for whatever reason," he added quickly, "where a phone is not pertinent—then perhaps a shotgun directional microphone is what you need." He placed another box in front of Mitch.

Mitch had heard of these. But he had never seen one.

"The unit also includes our HGA—High Gain Amplifier. It's constructed on a piece of PC board and housed along with its controls in an aluminum minibox. It's all solid state. These babies," he said, letting calculated enthusiasm creep into his voice, "can overhear a normal conversation over considerable distances. They can also hear through glass windows in houses or cars." He let that fact sink in. "These devices are used by law enforcement agencies. And," he added hastily, "serious-minded nature listeners."

"How much?" Mitch asked.

"Plans are $15.95. The kit here is $189.95. Fully assembled, tested and ready to go, it's $239.95."

Mitch was still thinking, weighing.

The salesman waited patiently.

"What have you got in the line of a homing or tracking device?"

Shifting gears, the salesman reached beneath the counter and produced a tiny, circular, metallic device. "It's magnetized. Emits a beeping tone that is picked up on a small, portable, pocket FM radio—also included. Range can be in excess of three kilometers, but it may vary due to terrain."

"And its price?"

"Plans are—"

"Just the fully assembled unit."

The salesman smiled. "$119.95."

It's all here, Mitch thought. All this stuff. Laser pistols, infrared viewers, voice scramblers, tesla coils, plasma generators, nuclear particle detectors, portable X-ray machines, ion generators, invisible alarm systems. And next door to this place is Home Hardware, and beside that is Bata Shoe Store, and then Duffy's Books and Japan One-Hour Photo. The future arrives as a franchise outlet, stemming the shock wave that should bowl us over.

"This stuff amazes me."

The salesman smiled at the unguarded comment, searching through his repertoire of anecdotes, stories, one-liners, for the appropriate level of retailer-consumer intimacy. "We even have a new existentialist roach spray."

He paused while Mitch frowned.

"It doesn't kill them. It fills them with self-doubt."

Mitch smiled in spite of himself. It was a good line.

He looked up. The salesman was smiling back.

"What's the newest thing you really do have?"

"In listening devices? Tracking devices?"

"Anything."

The man raised a finger into the air. "One minute." He appeared delighted at his success. Going into the room back of the counter, he reemerged seconds later with a carton larger than he had previously shown Mitch. "This," he said, "is the newest thing in stock."

"What is it?" There were only serial number markings on the top of the container.

The man opened the box at the top and lifted out two cylindrical plastic tanks; the nylon harness that housed them indicated that they were to be slung on one's back as a pair. Issuing from the tubes were separate rubber hoses that melded

into one, and at the end of that hose was a pistol-like apparatus.

"It's a water gun." The man set it out for display.

Mitch's skepticism was clear. He wasn't sure if this was yet
another example of the man's idiosyncratic humor.

"The tanks hold simple tap water that is forced out
through the nozzle," he indicated the pistol, "by a pump. The
water passes through a unit, which gives it an electrical
charge—a combination of direct and high frequency, alternating currents, at high voltages." Pointing again to the pistol,
he continued, "The nozzle has two openings and produces two
jets of water with opposite charges. If you direct the jets at a
plant, for instance, a current flows through the droplets that
fall on its leaves. A low current—less than a thousandth of an
ampere—stimulates growth. If the flow of current is increased
to five milliamps," he indicated a dial on the side of the pistol,
"the water will kill insects." He paused.

Mitch was puzzled. "So this is for gardening?"

The man raised an eyebrow. "The current can be adjusted
much higher."

Mitch looked back at the dial on the pistol's side. "How
high?"

"Well," he scratched the balding crown of his head,
"if you were to direct this stream at a human, then one or two
milliamps would be enough to constitute a 'sting mode.' A
'stun mode' would correspond to about twenty milliamps."

Mitch was beginning to understand.

"Could be used by riot forces to control crowds."

Mitch's mouth took on grim lines.

"The weapon is silent, and its operator would not have to
be a good shot because it sprays a wide beam of charged water."
He shrugged. "An automatic system could invariably be de-
vised."

Mitch picked up the pistol attachment and studied the
dial. "According to this, you can set it up over one hundred

milliamps. What would happen then?" He glanced at the sales-man's face.

The man shrugged again. "I guess that's what you'd call the 'kill mode.' "

Mitch's lips parted, then closed again. Lasers had begun to fossilize the science of ballistics. This just buried policing abilities deeper, he realized.

Donald Barbour. Elaine.

A vast haze of anger floated before his eyes. Then he touched the plastic nozzle, lifted the pistol-form in his hand, rolling his wrist slowly, feeling its lightness, and the anger passed, a fog lifting, replaced by cold resolve.

Why not? he thought. Mitch met the salesman's eyes.

"$249.95, ready to go."

Mitch spoke the word softly. "Deal."

The salesman smiled. "Just the water pistol? Or anything else?"

"I'll take the shotgun mike and the tracker as well."

"Quality material, all of it. Fully guaranteed." A pocket calculator appeared in his hand. For a few seconds his fingers worked the buttons, then he looked up. "Comes to $609.85. Plus tax." He let the figure sink in. "Visa, Mastercard, or American Express?"

"Cash," Mitch said, the darkness opening up inside him. He had come prepared.

That night Mitch had placed two of his new purchases inside a green, plastic garbage bag and, securing it with a twist-tie, had set it in the rear of his aging Chev's trunk.

Beside his car was Elaine's white Toyota. Newer than mine, he thought. Everybody's is newer than mine. Still on payments.

He found the trunk key for her car on his key ring, opened the trunk, and placed the magnetic tracking device inside the wheel well that housed the spare tire.

Slamming both lids, he stood back, letting the grayness of the underground parking lot surround him like a mist. He rolled his eyes upward and stared at the concrete-stippled ceiling.

Upstairs, he thought. My wife. My daughter.

The black hole inside him opened impossibly large, and moving toward the stairwell he had felt himself plunging into its lightless interior with unswerving singularity.

9 Standing on the porch of the semidetached house on Broadview Avenue, Mitch studied the peeling paint above him as he rang the bell.

He recognized her as soon as she opened the door. "Mrs. Wen?"

The woman nodded. Then he saw her recognize her own purse—its strap severed—in his hand. When she looked up to meet his face, he smiled gently and offered it to her.

Reflexively, she reached for it, snapping it open, scanning its interior.

"It's all there," he said.

Her hand checking the contents of the wallet, she met his gaze again. Her eyes softened. "Thank you. Thank you very much."

"My pleasure."

"How did you get it?"

"I'm a policeman. It's a long story."

She stepped aside. "Would you like to come in? Can I get you a cup of tea?" Her smile was broad now.

Over her shoulder, Mitch saw the plain kitchen at the end of the hall. Wind chimes tinkled delicately in a window. "No, thank you. I have to go."

She didn't seem to know what to say next. Then he saw her eyes move to his shoulder. "You're hurt," she said.

"I'm going to get it taken care of now." He turned and started down the steps.

"Officer?"

He stopped at the bottom of the stairs and turned around.
"I'd like to know your name." She bowed her head slightly.
He shook his head. "No," he said. "You wouldn't."

For a few brief seconds, he watched her accept this with
a stillness that was calming.

Then, bowing his head slightly in return, he got into his
car and left.

Beside him on the passenger seat were the two billfolds that
belonged to the two young thieves. Or should I call them mur-
derers? he wondered, remembering the shock of anger and
outrage that had accompanied the message delivered by the
Barking Dog.

There had been fourteen dollars in one and eleven dollars in the other. He had transferred the bills to the wallet in
Mrs. Wen's purse before returning it to her.

He turned left at Gerrard.

There was only one haven that he could think of right
now.

10

"The king's just reinforced his position as Britain's richest person." Paul Helwig frowned and stared as his son came through the door. "It was on the news at noon." His voice punctuated the last word sharply.

Mitch smiled and closed the door behind him.

"Sixty billion dollars. That's what they figure he's worth. Can you fuckin' believe it?"

"He can't take it with him."

"Trust funds. He'll set up trust funds for the other imbeciles."

"Like the Kennedys."

"Kennedy." The old man pondered. "At least old Joe made his own money."

"But his boys sure did have fun with it, didn't they?"

"Wally, at lunch." He was not to be sidetracked just yet. "Now there's one for you. He thinks he *deserves* his dough. Calls himself a monarchist." He shook his head. "Fuckin' ridiculous." He paused. "The guy still thinks he's in Vietnam when you talk to him. *That's* the kind of guy supports the king. Guy who's had his alleys scrambled by a howitzer."

Mitch had met old Wally. His father's description was pretty close.

"Second to the king is the duke of Westminster. Got about thirty billion."

Mitch sat down in the green armchair. "What about Paul

78

McCartney's estate? I always thought it was up there, soaring with the falcons."

"McCartneys?" Paul Helwig looked perplexed. "Barely makes the list. Only about a billion. Poor bastards." He gave his son a curious look. "You gotta be royalty."

Why am I even remotely surprised that he knows the McCartneys' worth? Mitch thought.

"You okay?" The weak eyes squinted.

"More or less. Got a sore shoulder."

"Try sleeping on the other side. Always works for me." He clicked the TV set off and sat quietly for a moment. "You know, I've been thinking about you and Elaine."

Mitch nodded. "Hard not to think about it, isn't it?"

"Age, experience," he said. "Supposed to give you wisdom."

His eyes traced the lines in his father's face. "Does it?"

"Good question. Age is one thing, experience another." He tilted his head, reflecting. "Amelia Gardener."

"Who?"

"She's certified by the Guinness Book of World Records as the world's oldest living person. One hundred and nineteen years old. We were talking about her Saturday, in the lounge, after dinner."

Mitch let him continue.

"No wisdom from her. She's senile. Lives in a nursing home in Palatka, Florida. Only been there five years. Before that, she spent seventy-nine years in an asylum—the Florida State Mental Hospital at Chattahoochee. Day after her thirty-fifth birthday, her husband committed her. So far as anyone can determine, he never saw her again."

"Jesus."

"She was hallucinating. Said she was killing her babies, but she didn't have any babies."

"Hallucinations don't mean she was crazy. Could have been lots of things. Could have been typhoid fever." Mitch found the story disturbing.

Paul Helwig shrugged. "Don't matter now. Hospital records of the time described her condition as 'post-thyroid psychosis,' a diagnosis doctors today don't even recognize."

It wasn't just the story itself that bothered Mitch. It was the realization that this was the kind of thing his father and these other old folks might sit around discussing.

"So you see," Paul Helwig said, "age by itself isn't much guarantee of anything." He digested his own tale. "Experience, though . . . " He sat back and folded his hands in his lap. The wry smile was back. "Yes, experience." He paused for dramatic effect. "Experience is what helps you recognize a mistake when you make it again."

Mitch smiled gratefully in return.

The lady who writes your checks for you, who sews buttons on for you," Mitch said.

"Flo."

"Yes, Flo." His father had introduced him to Flo only once, although he spoke of her often enough for Mitch to know that he had quite a soft spot for her.

"She's a kid. Still in her seventies. Eyes like a hawk though." He paused. "Nice lady."

"Is she in now?"

The old man looked at him like he was being smart. "Did you think maybe she was out partying? Of course she's in." He shook his head in disbelief. "Everybody here's always in."

"Could we call on her?"

Paul Helwig looked surprised. "What for?"

"My shoulder. I need somebody to look at it."

For the first time, the older man realized that there was something a little more serious about his son's shoulder than he had understood. He squinted, but his eyes couldn't make anything out. "You okay?" he asked.

"Just need some friendly hands to help." Then he added, "And eyes like a hawk."

The old man smiled. "Let's go then," he said, pushing himself up and out of the chair.

Flo Springer was seventy-two years old, to be exact, and had lived at Fellowship Towers for seven years. She had been widowed at fifty-eight, but had waited until she had become eligible for the old age pension before moving in. Her apartment was two floors above Paul Helwig's. When the senior Helwig had taken up residence there, she had studied him with interest, as she did all of the building's inhabitants. New arrivals underwent especially detailed scrutiny.

Paul Helwig had proved a particularly interesting case. Older than she would have preferred, but at least not a lifelong bachelor. They were the worst by far. He was even funny and made her laugh. And she had learned that that quality was one she should never dismiss too lightly, for the laughs were much fewer and farther between now than they ever had been. Nor did the future look much brighter.

They watched TV together, and he told her a million things, none of which made much sense to her. But they were always fascinating, and he seemed so deeply interested in so many areas. He restored some of her zest, and this made him more remarkable to her than ever, because she didn't have much zest left.

He had even brought a bottle of red wine up to her room on two different occasions, and, to her amazement, they had finished the whole thing each time. Once they had watched the Blue Jays play Baltimore. The other time they had watched a repeat of an ancient episode of *The Golden Girls*, and with the combination of the wine and the fact that he had talked nonstop all the way through it, she had no idea what the story had been about when she tried to recall it the next day.

Drinking was forbidden in the lease they all signed, so it had to be done discreetly. The number of empty bottles in the recycling closet every morning indicated that life was carrying on as usual for most of the Towers' residents.

So when she opened her door and saw Paul and his son standing there, she was both pleased and puzzled.

Not botherin' you, Flo?" Paul Helwig was genuinely solicitous.

"Why no, Paul. I was just watching television."

The old man looked at his son. "That's all we ever do around here."

Mitch looked sheepish at the comment.

"That or sleep," he added.

"Speak for yourself," she said, stepping back and motioning them inside.

"How're you, Mitch?" She smiled.

"Well, I could be better. Maybe you can even help." He waited a second while she digested this. "How've you been keeping?"

"Better'n I should. Why don't you two strays sit down. I'll put on the kettle. Make a pot of tea."

"That sounds terrific," Mitch said.

"Sleepin's okay," the older man said. "It's snorin' that'll kill you."

They both looked at him.

"Loud snorers starve their brains of oxygen."

Flo plugged the kettle in. Mitch just stared.

"Snorers are ten percent more likely than nonsnorers to suffer from nocturnal hypoxemia. It can reduce your level of intelligence."

Flo looked worried. Mitch smiled.

"You should hear the snorin' in the halls around here at night," he finished emphatically.

"Almond tea, raspberry, or plain?" asked Flo, opening the cupboard above the sink.

Mitch watched how she instantly reclaimed his father's

attention. The old man's face transformed at the thought of
such wondrous choices.

"Raspberry," he said, not letting Mitch get involved in a
question that was so clearly meant for him alone. "You know
how I love a cup of your raspberry tea."

They smiled a shared smile, and Mitch's mouth opened
slightly at the miracle of it all.

Very nasty," Flo said. "You need stitches."

Paul Helwig leaned closer, squinting.

"Yes, ma'am," Mitch said. "I'm sure I do."

"What happened?" the old man asked. "You get shot?"

"Not exactly." Mitch lifted his arm experimentally, then
rotated it carefully. "More like sliced."

"Christ," the old man said. Then he looked at Flo. "It's
bein' a cop. It's getting ridiculous."

"I can't stitch it for you, Mitch. You must know that."

"Just cleaned and bandaged tightly will do, Flo. I'd really
appreciate it."

They both stared at her. She stared back, clearly perplexed.

"I need two good hands to do it, Flo. Can't do it by myself." Sensing the questions behind her hesitation, Mitch was
about to reassure her when his father spoke up.

"Do you know who Curious George is?"

They turned to look at him.

"He's a one-hundred-twenty-kilogram alligator snapping
turtle at the Metro Zoo. Biggest one of its type in captivity.
They figure he's about fifty years old. Couple of years ago they
discovered hundreds of pieces of lead scattered throughout his
head, along with a fifteen-centimeter fishhook."

"This has a point, I trust," Mitch said.

"I have hydrogen peroxide, some gauze, some tape," said
Flo.

"I think that'll do it." Mitch winced at the throbbing brought on by the tentative movements he'd just tried.

Flo disappeared into the bathroom.

"He's been hooked and shot, but still manages to waddle around. Vets have picked dozens of pellets out of him, but they can't get 'em all. Every once in a while, these pellets flare up and cause an infection. George goes off his food. Then they got to dig a couple more out."

Mitch raised an eyebrow.

"He's like you."

"Like me."

"Yeah. You and George. You both been shot, but you're both still kickin' around. Tough."

Flo returned with dressings and bandaging, and Mitch relaxed.

Tough, he thought. Me and George. But he wasn't sure. He wasn't sure at all. Running through his head were a limping army of faces that didn't make him feel so tough. He saw Elaine and Donald Barbour, Mario and Angela Ciracella and little Tony, Sam Karoulis.

And Barbie.

Closing his eyes, he felt himself swollen with lead pellets and fishhooks that would never come out, unless he exploded, spraying everyone around him.

And he knew then why Curious George, even under his armor, moved with such care.

Flo Springer's sudden touch on his skin was a healing balm.

TWO

Meanwhile, of the broken keel of Ahab's wrecked craft the carpenter made him another leg.

—Herman Melville
Moby Dick

11

"I liked my old desk, Huziak. It's as simple as that." Karoulis sat back and slumped in the chair.

"It's gone, Captain. Better get used to it."

"Why do I have to get used to everything?"

The two days since the explosion had turned both their worlds upside down. But the job went on. Nothing stopped it. Down the hall from the makeshift office where they were sitting, the hammering and construction of carpentry and repairs was in full progress.

I'll have to get used to that too, he thought. Goddamn noise everywhere.

Sitting opposite him, Huziak crossed his legs, opening the fat file folder on his lap as he did so. "We've got some beautiful stuff this morning, Captain."

"The station gets blown apart." He shrugged. "Carry on, they say. Do your best."

Huziak took the first sheet from the file. "Arrested a guy at Pearson International last night as he stepped off a flight from California. Charged with kidnapping his former girlfriend in North York. Woman claims that he forced her to go with him by bus to Buffalo, threatening to kill her family if she didn't cooperate. They then took a flight to Los Angeles and she said it was two days before she could escape. She returned home, suspect was arrested and not charged, and yesterday Los Angeles police put him on a flight to Toronto. We charged him. Guy's twenty-nine. Lives in Thornhill."

"What we do for love."

"We're looking for a guy wearing a wig who robbed three stores downtown yesterday. There's an accomplice. We've got descriptions."

"Next."

"Staff at Chopsticks on Danforth were forced into the basement by two armed bandits and robbed of cash and jewelry. They also took money from the cash register." He scanned down the report. "Described as Orientals aged about twenty-five; five six, hundred and sixty pounds."

Karoulis's face did not change expression.

Huziak shuffled through the papers, extracting one farther down. "We laid twenty-nine charges in the auto insurance scam."

Karoulis reflected on the case. About thirty percent of the more than 140,000 annual stolen car reports in the city were phony. People just got rid of their cars on their own or hired middlemen to dispose of them before filing a stolen car report.

"Quite a collection of individuals. A teacher, a parks worker, a restaurant manager, nurses, housewives, construction workers—"

"The usual demographically diverse cross section, no doubt," said Karoulis.

"That's one way of putting it."

"You know I can't take it all."

Huziak smiled. "I know."

"Highlight 'em for me. What're the really good ones?"

Huziak pulled a handful of reports from the file and sat back. "There's one here about a guy who was kidnapped, tortured, glued and feathered, and locked in a cage with vicious dogs. Guy escaped."

Karoulis said nothing.

"Passerby spotted him as he ran naked and screaming up Shaw Street. Guy's hair was cut off, eyebrows shaved, rubbed all over with glue. Burn marks on his body, even on his genital area, caused by a stun gun. They'd told this guy they were going to drive him up into Algonquin Park and leave him there for dead, for the animals to eat."

"Sounds to me like he was already with the animals. What was this all about?"

Huziak studied the report. "It's listed as a 'long-standing business dispute over money.' Owner of the house on Shaw and four others have been booked on suspicion of kidnapping." He paused, reading more. "They found a live alligator, a frozen alligator, a rattlesnake, two scorpions, and five dogs at the house."

Why, thought Karoulis, am I surprised at anything that I hear anymore?

"At Marine Terminal Fifty-One, Port of Toronto, foot of Cherry Street, they seized a shipment of fish stuffed with three million dollars' worth of cocaine. Seven people detained."

Fish, thought Karoulis. Of course, fish. "What kind?"

Huziak looked up. "Kind of what?"

"Fish."

Reading further, Huziak smiled. "Red porgy," he said.

"We've found drugs in coconuts, shoes, even miniature cribs used in Christmas nativity scenes." Karoulis's tone waffled between world-weary and angry. "Why not red porgy?" Clearly, there was a point where nothing made sense anymore, no matter how you tried to see it. They were close to that point.

"One more? The Far Side of crime?" Huziak paused.

"You've been saving this one."

Huziak shrugged.

"Let's have it."

"Story's making the rounds this morning. Happened last night out in Peel."

Karoulis waited.

"Peel police were called out to the Derrydale golf club at three A.M. They nabbed a four-man gang in a nine-foot-deep pond, equipped with scuba gear and underwater lights. They seized fourteen hundred golf balls, which the divers had loaded into floating plastic tubs."

Man's ability to devise new wrinkles in the crime fabric is limitless, thought Karoulis.

"They were charged with trespassing and theft."

"The trespassing I can see. The theft I'm not so clear on."

"According to English Common Law, once an object is abandoned by its original owner, it becomes the property of the landowner."

"How did you know this?"

"I didn't. But the golf club owners sure did. They got a contract with a firm that retrieves balls for resale. This company apparently retrieves five thousand balls a week from Glen Abbey course alone, polishes them like eggs, then sells them to large chain stores like Canadian Tire, Zellers, Woolco. It's big business." Huziak smiled. "Every now and then, they find a whole set of clubs down there. Even a golf cart."

I can never play golf again, knowing this, Karoulis thought. All I'd be able to see is the bottoms and walls of the ponds blanketed with balls. He stared at Huziak. "The world is nuts, Huziak."

Huziak's eyebrows went up and he nodded. "Seems like it."

From down the hall, the whine of an electric saw slicing the end off a spruce two-by-four cut the air, and Karoulis felt yet one more shard of illusion clatter to the floor with the severed end.

Mitch and Elaine Helwig have separated," said Karoulis, watching Huziak shuffle the files in his folder back into order.

The sergeant stopped and looked up at him. A silence fell before he answered. "I didn't know."

"No," he said. "Nobody knew. He didn't tell anybody."

Huziak remained quiet.

"I just found out myself." He wanted a cigarette. He wanted to pace. Anything. "Fuck it," he said finally. "Fuck it all."

Huziak sighed, shook his head.

"Did I ever tell you that I was married once before?" Karoulis lifted his eyes to Huziak's face without moving his head.

Huziak nodded. "You did, Captain."

"The breakup just about killed me."

Huziak just listened.

"Just about fucking killed me." And then Karoulis too was silent.

12

"It's me."

"Oh." Elaine flicked on the video so that she could see his face while she talked with him on the phone.

Mitch licked his lips. He was nervous. "I've got a place. Small. But it'll do."

She said nothing.

"I want to see Barbie."

"Maybe she doesn't want to see you."

"She needs to see me. You know that. Don't get crazy."

Elaine said nothing for a few seconds. Then: "I've got a lawyer. You get one too."

"For Christ's sake, Elaine. Those bastards will just pit us against one another. It'll get worse, not better. We can work this out by ourselves."

"You get one too," she repeated.

The coldness in her voice chilled him. Like a wave of nausea, the nightmare of his situation was continuing to grow. He fought down the adrenaline surge that accompanied her words. "What about Barbie?" he asked, forcing the dialogue back to his daughter. He studied his estranged wife's face, the anger in her features glowing even in the weak, gray image before him.

Elaine sighed heavily, put her hand to her forehead, seemed to think. "What did you have in mind?"

"This weekend, for starters. I'd pick her up Friday, after school, bring her back Sunday evening." He paused. "Then we can talk about something more regular, work out some routines."

"Suppose I don't want routines. Suppose I think you should just go away, disappear." Her anger was still there, smoldering.

He remained calm. For half an hour before calling, he'd drummed up the worst dialogue scenarios that he could imagine in his head, preparing for just this kind of madness. "It doesn't work that way," he said. "Lawyers or no lawyers, it's not what you want or what I want that's going to happen anymore. We have to think of her."

"I think you're crazy. I think you're dangerous."

Mitch watched her eyes blaze, realizing that she was going to displace onto him all the rage and frustration that she had been accumulating like a poison, right here and now, if he let this go any further, let himself get drawn into her vortex. The pull was real, a swirl of madness rising like a hot wind from a volcanic pit, and he fought against it.

"Daddy?"

His daughter's face appeared suddenly beside Elaine's, her unexpected smile pulling him back from the edge. His heart melted, and just for a moment, a very brief moment, life made sense again.

I *think you're crazy. I think you're dangerous.*

The sentences rang in his head like gunshots after he had finally made the arrangements. Barbie's appearance had been a boon for him, since Elaine had been reluctant to engage in further confrontation with her there, and he had let Elaine's accusations go unchallenged.

But alone now, in his apartment, the ceilings sloping down

around him on both sides, he calmed himself and remembered why she had said those things to him.

She had said them because they had once been true.

He remembered the madness. He remembered, two days after Huziak had handed him the brown envelope with Donald Barbour's name, address and phone number, what he had done.

It seemed impossible, in hindsight. Mitch found himself hovering on the edge of psychological denial, almost unwilling to accept his own memories.

Sitting down in the wicker chair, he rolled his eyes up to stare through the skylight. It was night, and he could see nothing there.

Nothing at all.

Only the black hole of memory.

I think you're crazy. I think you're dangerous.

He remembered.

He had phoned in sick, that's what he had done. It was something that he had never done before.

Lying in bed that morning, he had heard Elaine showering and the muffled sounds of Barbie dressing and playing in her room. He lay beneath the covers like an uncoiled whip waiting to be snapped, his brain a frenzy, a shifting, riotous kaleidoscope of hots and colds, blacks and whites, fears and angers.

She came into the room in her robe, with a towel wrapped around her hair. While rummaging through the closet, laying out clothes on the foot of the bed, she spoke to him. "You awake?"

He rolled over, feigned pulling himself up from the depths of sleep. "What time is it?"

"Seven-twenty."

"Mm."

"You're on three-to-eleven shift again, right?"

"Mm."

"And tomorrow?"

"Same." His skin was prickling.

"Okay." She rubbed her scalp under the towel. "Mrs. Chan will be here at three for Barbie. She'll be making dinner for her and staying here till I get home. I've got to work late again."

His mouth went dry.

"New account. Stuff to clean up," she added.

He asked nothing.

"Go to sleep. I'll see you later."

He lay with his eyes closed, listening to the sounds of her dressing. In the kitchen, he could hear Barbie pouring Cheerios into a bowl, the refrigerator door opening and closing. He didn't need a Barking Dog. His feet and hands felt cold, and he could hear his heart pounding in his ears.

He lay there, waiting for them both to leave.

Waiting for his heart to stop pounding. Waiting for a warmth that wouldn't come.

He was alone in the apartment by 8:15. Elaine would drop Barbie at Thorncliffe Park public school before heading north and east to the Nishiyama building on Markham Road where she had worked for the past six years.

He phoned the station, looked into the vidphone, told his lie. He hung up.

It had seemed easy.

But he was shaking.

In his mind, as if from a great height, he saw Elaine's white Toyota inching like a blind beetle along its flat, fixed route.

It was 5:30 P.M.

Mitch had been waiting in the parking lot at Nishiyama

for an hour before he saw Donald Barbour emerge and get into his car—a dark green Mazda sports coupe. He remained motionless and inconspicuous, slouched down behind the wheel of his Chev, watching the vehicle pull out of the lot and slide into the traffic heading south.

He watched the red taillights dwindle and disappear.

Then he resumed waiting.

Elaine had been telling some of the truth about working late. She finally came out of the building at 6:30 P.M., got into her white Toyota, and like Donald Barbour and so many others he had witnessed in the last hour, slid uneventfully into the flow of traffic.

On the seat beside him, Mitch clicked on the small, portable pocket FM radio that he had purchased at Guardian Intelligence and Protective Services.

It began to beep rhythmically. He lowered the volume.

He gazed blankly out into the stream of headlights that had sprung up with the fall of evening, listening to the regularity of the signal beside him, as if in a dream.

My heartbeat, he thought.

It pulsed steadily.

He sat for a moment longer, letting his life throb with quiet urgency, before starting his engine and blending into the southbound traffic.

She was about a dozen cars ahead of him, and they drove for more than thirty minutes, down Markham Road to Kingston Road, then southwest into the city. At Dundas she turned west, and Mitch followed the blur of taillights and the steady volume of beeps until he saw her turn south at Sherbourne. At Front Street, she turned west again.

Their apartment, with Barbie and Mrs. Chan, was miles to the northeast.

Just before Jarvis Street she turned into a municipal parking lot on the south side of Front. Mitch pulled over to the curb and watched her jockey the Toyota into a vacant slot.

The beeping continued on the seat beside him.

He saw her get out of the car and walk north to Front Street. She crossed not less than a hundred meters away and headed into the restaurant directly opposite: the Charles Bistro.

In the cool interior darkness of his own car, Mitch reached over and clicked off the FM beeps. The silence, so sudden, let him hear his own breathing, deep and troubled.

His eyes scanned the parking lot that she had just left, searching. It was there.

The dark green Mazda sports coupe.

Mitch's eyes flashed back to the restaurant's masquerading surface design, quaint and twentieth century.

He started the Chev, moved it closer along the curb so that he had a direct, unobstructed line of sight toward its facade, parked it again, turned off the engine. Then he picked up the earphones from the seat beside him and adjusted them on his head, straightening the wires that ran to the solid-state aluminum box. Beside it, the shotgun directional mike lay waiting. Mitch picked it up, hefted it, and as he aimed it at the restaurant's exterior and adjusted the dials on the aluminum box, his heart began to hammer wildly.

Donald Barbour watched Elaine Helwig come through the door and caught her eye. After a quick word of explanation, she followed the headwaiter to the table and allowed herself to be seated.

"You shouldn't work so late." He attempted a smile.

Elaine seemed flustered, meeting his eyes only briefly. Her fingers fussed with the cutlery and napkin, straightening, arranging.

"I shouldn't be here," she said.

He said nothing to this. Don Barbour, forty-five years of age, married for eighteen of those years, father of two teenagers, touched his mustache with the index finger of his right hand instead of speaking. If the advertising world had been seeking a stereotypical WASP male for a model, it might have begun and ended its search with him.

"But you are here. Enjoy yourself. It's the end of the day."

"You can't call me anymore." Elaine tried to meet his eyes strongly.

"I want to call you."

"You can't."

"Just because your husband answered once—"

"No. Not just because of that."

They were interrupted by the appearance of a waiter.

Elaine became quiet, regaining composure.

He sensed his opening and sought to wedge it apart wider. "It *is* the end of the day. You have to eat something. So do I. Order something. We'll dine. Try to be civilized." He waited. "And we'll talk it out."

She met his eyes.

"I promise. We'll talk," he said.

She sighed, nodded consent, and opened the menu.

Donald Barbour felt the warm glow of the business deal that had begun to simmer.

Alone in the dead stillness of the Chev's interior, Mitch Helwig sat, frozen, wired to aluminum and copper, his hand clutching the steel aimed at the Charles, his eyes vacant, his mouth slightly ajar, as the words trickled through filament, cascaded among electrons into the depths of his skull and soul, scalding him with the purity and sting of quicksilver.

I'm dying, he thought. Surely to God I'm dying.

Elaine had ordered the filet of sole, feeling like something light, but then had eaten ravenously. And against her better judgment, she had allowed Don to order a carafe of white wine.

Against my better judgment, she thought. I'm beginning to think I've lost whatever better judgment I may ever have had.

Now, as he emptied the last of the wine into their glasses, she sat back. The talk thus far had been uneventful, circuitous.

And the food and drink, at the end of a working day, had made her mellower.

"I'm sorry," he said at last, "about the other night. My call was foolish, indiscreet."

She studied him. "It was more than foolish or indiscreet. It was an embarrassment, an invasion into my privacy. You called my home." She shook her head disbelievingly. "How would you like me calling your home and having Ruth answer?"

He dropped his eyes, conceding this.

"I told you that day, and I'm repeating it loud and clear now: it's over. Finished. It was a mistake."

"It wasn't a mistake. That's why I called."

"It was a mistake." She gathered her thoughts, wondering whether to continue. "The first time should have been the last time we were together. I don't know how this has continued."

But she did know how it had continued. It had continued because she was vulnerable. Because she needed someone. Because her husband was a cop and had become fully entangled in the web of his own world, losing his own perspective.

And because this man opposite her had been persistent.

She watched him reach across and place his hand atop hers. She saw his proficiency, his concerned contact, his soft sell without words. And temporarily, it worked. She relaxed. She did not encourage his touch, but neither did she withdraw from it.

He smiled.

Elaine watched her hand covered beneath his and recognized the potential turning point. But she couldn't bring herself to act, couldn't bring herself to accept or withdraw; she could only remain frozen, afraid of the future as much as she was of the present, as much as she both regretted and cherished the past.

She glanced up at Don. It was actually simple to stay with him in this floating relationship, without analysis, without commitment. And so impossible.

But they were here, now.

Carefully, she withdrew her hand at last and drank the last of her wine.

"I know a piano bar within walking distance," he said.

"I don't think so."

"What's the harm?"

She shrugged. "And then what?"

He shrugged back. "And then we'll see."

And then we'll see, she thought. But she couldn't see. Couldn't see at all.

Mitch slammed the door of the Chev behind him and, while crossing Front Street to the parking lot, unfolded the telescopic shoulder-stock of the Sanyo laser, shrugging it into the nook between his chest and biceps. The darkness of the evening kept him inconspicuous, as did the absence of pedestrians.

When he had reached the green Mazda sports coupe, he raised the twenty-five-centimeter, black plastic barrel of the weapon and aimed it at the front of the vehicle. Methodically, he squeezed the trigger, sweeping it across the windshield, and the flare of searing blue light sliced the glass with a frying crackle. When he swept the beam across the car's roof, the metal parted as if he had pulled opened a zipper, and smoke began to billow upward. He continued his vivisection, trashing the upholstery.

"Hey!"

Mitch glanced sideways.

The parking lot attendant began to say something else, saw the madness in the face of the man wielding the laser, and thought better of it. Instead, he slid out of his booth and scuttled away.

Mitch turned back to the green Mazda and exploded each tire in turn.

Everyone in the Charles heard the four explosions, but no one was curious enough to go outside to learn their source.

Elaine frowned across the table at Don. Like everyone else, they glanced toward the windows, but there was nothing to be seen except their own reflections.

Mitch strode toward the white Toyota. His eyes were watery as they dilated in the smoking darkness. Randomly, he swept the barrel of the Sanyo back and forth across the unpaid-for vehicle, watching it die a bubbling, charred, motionless death, cracking it like an egg. As the glass collapsed inward and the roof parted, he saw a pair of Elaine's gloves, an umbrella. The sight of one of Barbie's books in the backseat seemed to snap him back and he released the trigger, blinking.

He stood over the mutilated metal carcass, trying to focus, trying to stop his heart from slamming inside his chest, trying to stop his shaking. Gulping the cool night air, mixed with the taste of carbon and chrome, as if it were a liquor, he tried to intoxicate himself into a merciful oblivion.

Then without any conscious thought, he stepped back and raised the laser rifle and proceeded to explode the four tires of her car as well.

The noise deafened him, and the smoke, foul and thick, billowed in serpentine coils upward into the starless sky.

This time, the four new explosions sent several people cautiously out onto nearby apartment balconies to see what was happening. A few people filtered out onto the street from the two local restaurants as well.

Elaine Helwig stood on the sidewalk beside Donald Barbour and stared in horror at the scene.

It came to her in a thunderclap.

Mitch, she thought.

Her eyes scanned the devastation.

But he was nowhere to be seen.

Mitch had not gone home that night. After driving aimlessly for an hour, he found himself on Mount Pleasant Road, north of St. Clair, the vast Mount Pleasant Cemetery flanking him on either side.

It hit him where he was.

He slowed, made a U-turn, headed south, then made a right onto Moore Avenue, where he pulled over, parked, and got out. The houses here backed onto the cemetery, and a stroll down a few of the driveways finally revealed a fence that he could climb with a minimum of difficulty into the locked acreage.

Once within, even in the dark, he knew the way.

He found Mario Ciracella's headstone and sat down in front of it on the damp, cool grass. He enjoyed the moments of memory and solace he found with his partner, his friend, who had been killed so senselessly, leaving his life, his wife and son, behind.

Leaving him behind.

The fifteen-minute visit was soothing. The dead, thought

Mitch, ask so little. What are the debts? Why the pain? How should we live?

When he had calmed himself, he rose and stared off into the darkness. The other headstone was about ten minutes away. He could find it, too, without sight.

It was beside his mother's grave that he had slept that night.

13 Karoulis was spending Friday evening watching the Cubs play the Marlins on the Sports Network—a game in which he had no emotional involvement whatsoever—when the phone beeped.

Poor fuckin' Florida, he thought, as Gonzales, their first baseman, fanned for the second time that evening, ending the sixth inning. They'll never get out of the basement.

When he picked up the receiver, Mitch Helwig's face appeared on the screen. After their chat beneath Mitch's skylight, he had wondered if Mitch would call him. "Stranger. How are ya?"

"Doing good," Mitch said.

"It's six–nothing for the Cubs. The Marlins must depress all those old people in Miami. I think the old people are sellin' them their Valium."

"You goin' to Florida when you retire, Captain?"

"And watch the Marlins? Gimme a break. What can I do for you? Been meanin' to call. Got no time, though. Gotta watch the Marlins. You know how it is."

"I know how it is. Listen, I've been thinking about your offer—your patio chairs and table. I really could use them. Especially this weekend. I'm picking up Barbie early tomorrow, taking her back to school Monday morning. Could I come by and pick them up?"

"On one condition."

Mitch waited.

"You help clean out my basement. Take what you need." He smiled. "I'll put a couple of beers in the freezer. It'll save me from watchin' some poor bastard come out of the Marlins' bullpen next inning. Get over here."

Mitch smiled. "Thanks."

Mitch had been to Sam Karoulis's house only once before—when the older man had aligned with him against the Archangel, making the Honda prototype skimmer available to him and authorizing the hit on the warehouse.

It seemed like another lifetime.

The house was on Glen Manor Drive in the Beaches, no more than five minutes from Mitch's apartment. With the ravine and parklike surroundings, the area was a civilized oasis in the city: curving streets and older, detached homes—leaded windows, some ivy—dating mostly from the early twentieth century. Nice, Mitch thought, gazing up at the house from his car. Must be nice. His third-floor apartment sprang up in contrast in his head, as did the Thorncliffe complex where he used to live. Other worlds. He pictured Barbie playing in the area and closed his eyes.

The engine of the Chev chugged and banged a few extra turns after he cut the ignition.

Karoulis answered the door almost immediately after Mitch pressed the doorbell. Stepping aside, he gestured to the TV that could be heard in the living room. "Eight–nothing for the Cubs."

Mitch smiled.

"C'mon in."

As Mitch entered, a woman that he judged to be in the nebulous area of her forties appeared on the stairs from the second floor. She was dark-haired, tiny, and trim. When she arrived at the bottom, she extended her hand. "I'm Helen."

"Mitch."

Her hand was firm, her eyes warm.

"Sam's talked about you," she said.

"Only in his sleep, I'm sure. I can hear him muttering and cursing now."

"You'd be surprised," she said.

Karoulis interrupted. "Downstairs is where the treasures are. We should go down and start diggin'. I'll get those two beer. You want one, Helen?"

"Thanks, no. You mind if I switch from the ball game to something else?"

"Please do. Put the Marlins out of their misery."

Before she left, she put her hand on Mitch's arm. "Please, Mitch. Take whatever he offers. Do clean out the basement."

Karoulis looked at Mitch. "What'd I tell you?" he said. Then he headed into the kitchen.

Karoulis dragged the round plastic tabletop from a dusty corner in the basement, rolled it out into the clear and propped it against a steel support pillar. Then he went back into the same corner and pulled out a plastic bag with the four legs inside. He tore the bag apart and took them out, examining each one in turn. "They slip right into slots on the bottom of the table." He held one forth. "This one's got an adjustable foot," he demonstrated by screwing it in and out, "so the table won't wobble." He glanced back into the dusty corner. "I don't think you'll want the umbrella that fits in the center." He looked back at Mitch. "Will you?"

"Not today. Maybe when I start entertaining."

Karoulis stood back, looking off into the shadows of the basement's other corners. "Lots of stuff down here. Probably house another family forever. Basements. Scary."

He watched Mitch studying the adjustable foot of the table leg, reflecting on the forces that had brought him here, to this basement, to start his life again with plastic.

"When I first started on the force, I came across a couple

that had lived together in silence for twelve years," Karoulis said.

Mitch looked up at him.

"Not only didn't they speak to each other in all that time, they even discussed getting a divorce by exchanging notes." He took a long sip from his beer, the bottle cool against his lips.

"Patricia and Robert Benzinger. That was their names. I still remember." He paused. "Hard to forget."

Mitch was silent for a moment. Then he asked, "Friends?"

"Naw. Nothin' like that. I was the cop sent to arrest her after she admitted stealing twenty bucks from the restaurant where she worked. It all came out in court. I just sat there and listened, amazed. Her lawyer said she began stealing money after her husband stopped giving her cash and because she was depressed about her domestic life. Said she had given her husband a note saying she intended to file for divorce, and he returned it with 'go ahead' written on it." He stared at Mitch. "So it could be worse."

"What happened?"

"What happened? She was fined two hundred bucks and ordered to pay two hundred and fifty in compensation to the restaurant." He picked at the label on the bottle in his hand. "And they got divorced." He shrugged. "That's what happened."

Mitch took a swig of his own beer. "Sounds sad."

"It was. It was also ridiculous. People can be nuts. Especially in a marriage. You gotta fight to stay sane." He looked at Mitch. "Right?"

Mitch remembered the sounds of exploding tires, saw the nightmare of smoke boiling upward from the past. "Right," he said.

Karoulis was dragging a large, dust-covered cardboard box from the back of a shelf. Lurching it into his arms, he placed it on the basement floor and began to pull off the tape that sealed it up. When he opened it, he thrust aside fistfuls of balled-up newspaper and lifted out a couple of dinner plates. A pattern of blue flowers and birds rimmed their edge. He held them out to Mitch. "Take them. The whole box. Please. Get them the hell out of here. They been here forever. Nobody uses 'em." He probed down in the bottom of the box. "There's cutlery down at the bottom. You're in business."

"Where'd you get this stuff?"

"Who knows. Basements. Stuff just grows in 'em. It's a mystery."

"I can't just take it—"

"You heard Helen. You heard me. Take it. We don't want it. Christ," he said, building, "get a truck. Take the whole fuckin' place." He waved his arm around expansively. "Instant happiness. That is," a half-smile appeared, "unless you've already got your pattern registered at Birk's. Or the table don't go with the wallpaper you've got picked out." He stared him down. "Is that it?"

Mitch smiled, began to nod. "I'll cancel the wallpaper," he said.

"Good."

Need towels?"

Mitch hesitated, then gave in. "Sure."

"Got these. Given to us by Helen's sister." He took down a shopping bag from a shelf, pulled out a dark wine-colored bath towel with silver satin flowers stitched onto the edging, and showed it to him. "There's a whole set in here." He flipped it to glance at the label. "One hundred percent cotton." He shrugged. "Can you go wrong?"

Mitch took the bag from him. "Not at all."

"Give your bathroom a bit of pizazz. Babes will go wild when they see 'em. Think you're a pistol." He eyed Mitch for a second before asking: "Any other woman?"

Mitch shook his head.

Karoulis nodded. "Good. Makes it easier to decorate then. Carte blanche, and taste is no object." He rolled his head back, thinking. "I remember one other one."

"One other what?"

"Case involving a husband and a wife. A classic in the department. Guy in his late sixties, pourin' his daily oatmeal into a bowl for breakfast. When he added milk, these brown specks started floatin' around on top. Became suspicious. Wouldn't eat it. Later that day, he finds signs of a break-in the previous night. Turns out his ex-wife, sixty-seven years old, broke into the home and sprinkled rat poison in the oatmeal box. They'd been divorced about two years, but had been married for thirty-seven years before that. The ex was bitter over the divorce and upset over the old guy's plans to remarry." He shook his head, folded the towel and replaced it in the bag. "Hell hath no fury . . . "

Mitch took another sip of his beer. "I got no friends," he said suddenly.

Karoulis looked at him without speaking. The confidence had been imparted with such simplicity and candor that it left little room for response.

Mitch's face was starkly lit and lined by the basement's bare lightbulbs, the geometry of loss sketched there.

"I remember," Karoulis said simply.

"Mario was my friend. He's gone."

Karoulis said nothing.

"Got no brothers or sisters." A pause. "Got my father, though."

"I remember," said Karoulis, "how I lost friends. People make judgments. Figure you must have done something wrong. They resented and envied me simultaneously. Mostly, they resented the fact that I'd upset the patterns they were living by. Nobody stood by me unconditionally. I made them nervous. Especially other couples we'd known together." He was quiet for a moment. "I remember one lady I met at a Christmas party shortly after I separated from my first wife. After talking with me for a half hour or so, she then proceeded to tell me why my wife had gotten rid of me. That was the way she phrased it—as if that was the way it had happened and she could know such a thing. That was the point at which I realized that I'd entered a limbo that was not comprehensible to anyone who hadn't been there. Yet they were all still going to comprehend it, apply their own structures, values, theories."

Karoulis tipped his beer back against his lips, finished the bottle. "The self-righteous are a tough audience," he said. "There was a lot of smirking behind my back by some so-called friends. I remember stumbling onto that too." He began to poke at other dust-covered cartons along the shelf from which he'd just taken down the towels. "Listened to a lawyer who practiced family law at another Christmas party a couple of years later—" he looked at Mitch "—fuckin' Christmas parties . . . fuckin' lawyers too . . . who described his clients as the 'crazies.' He held forth while his wife sat in the other room. I chatted with her for a few minutes. Enough minutes for me to know how full of shit the guy was. This was a lady who could see right through his bombast and rant. It was pretty clear he was living the modern classical domestic self-delusion."

Mitch was listening, appreciating. There was a lot that he needed to hear, and Karoulis obviously knew this.

"You'll see hypocrisy and revisionism everywhere in your so-called friends." Karoulis lifted down another carton, tearing at the aged tape holding it shut. "But," he looked at Mitch, "you'll get smarter. You'll be wiser. It's a hell of a character builder. If," he added, "you live through it."

They stared at one another.

"You'll live through it."

Mitch didn't answer. He couldn't see the future.

"I'll help you," said Karoulis.

There were pots and pans in the newly opened box.

"Instant kitchen," said Karoulis, standing back from it. "You'll be cooking like a wild man soon."

Mitch lifted a pot from the carton and turned it over in his hand like it was an exotic weapon.

"It's called a pot, Helwig. You put it on the stove. Put somethin' in it. It's a miracle of modern science."

"Now I got to start shopping, right?"

"Buy some soup. Start slow. Don't strain yourself."

"What happened to Maria when your marriage broke up?" asked Mitch.

"Maria." Karoulis appeared to let the word wash him with memories, emotions. "I let her mother keep custody of her. She was only eleven at the time, and I didn't know much about little girls. Don't know much about big ones either," he added. "Seemed like the right thing to do at the time. I was moving out. The guy always seems to move out, right?" He looked at Mitch. "And she had her friends and her school pretty much established. And I had my own guilt to deal with. It's like you're lost, and taking a kid with you when you're lost didn't seem smart. You know what I mean?"

Mitch nodded.

"But I was wrong. It was a mistake."

Mitch stared at him now.

"A big mistake." His voice was firm.

"Why?"

"Didn't see her enough. Every other weekend for a year, then every weekend for two years after that. When she turned fourteen, she pretty much came and went between my ex and me as she pleased. By sixteen, things were really good, and I'd remarried. She was around more than half the time. Helen and she got along great. But," his eyes wandered into the dark corners of the basement, "for those first three years, my rope was jerked pretty good. Her mother set all the conditions and I just had to live with them. It was a power thing. Punitive." He paused. "And I didn't understand how much I needed her. Maria. I missed her till I hurt." He looked at Mitch again. "It was a mistake."

Mitch was quiet for a moment. Then he asked, "What should I do?"

"Joint custody. Get it in writing. As soon as possible.

Forget the furniture, the stereo, all that shit that people fight over. It's all bullshit. Joint physical and legal shared custody. Half the time with you, half with Elaine. That's the name of the game when both parents are good parents."

It was a new idea to Mitch.

"Let Barbie be with you half the time. Let her see what's involved in setting up your life again. Let her see what you go through on a day-to-day basis. Don't make your life a mystery to her. And don't let yourself be made into the bad guy. Enough of those other people I was tellin' you about will do that for you. Make her number one and things will start shifting back into place. Take her to school in the morning. Make her lunches. Have dinner together. Have her friends over."

Mitch was still holding the pot, thinking.

"Bang yourself on the forehead with that pot, Helwig. Wake yourself up. I'll get us two more cool brews." He headed for the stairs.

Halfway up, he turned around. "Mitch," he said.

Mitch met his eyes.

"I'm your friend," he said. Then he continued up the stairs.

It was 10:30 P.M. when Mitch, his car stuffed with everything Sam and Helen Karoulis could give him, was stopped at a red light at Greenwood and Queen. He saw it in the window of a variety store on the north side.

He pulled to the curb, parked, and went in. He didn't even dicker with the $29.95 asking price. The Chinese saleslady smiled warmly as she got it out of the window for him.

He had plates and cups with blue flowers and birds, wine-colored towels with silver satin flowered edging, gray plastic outdoor table and chairs, dented pots and pans with the copper bottoms worn away, a box of mismatched glasses, cups and mugs, a pile of worn, frayed, multicolored blankets, and a mattress with a mysterious purple stain in its center—with the label "Orthopedic Morning Glory" stitched into its corner— tied across the car's roof.

The gold-painted, plaster bust of Elvis that he had just purchased would fit right into his new life.

He smiled, pleased with himself.

14

The man sitting in the black Buick up the street from the Karoulis home on Glen Manor withdrew a small pocket calendar from his jacket and jotted down the time that Mitch Helwig drove away. He had watched as the police captain helped Helwig fasten a sagging mattress to the car's roof and tuck various boxes into the trunk and backseat. He let Helwig make a right turn onto Queen Street before he started his own vehicle, trailing slowly and patiently behind him.

In his office, Deputy Chief of Police Joseph Galecki finished reading the newspaper account of the station bombing, which included brief excerpts from his press conference. Nothing there really. No leads of any significance. Then he noted the hysteria about the latest provincial budget targeting the deficit—via increased taxes, as usual. The piece about the California firm marketing solar-powered tombstones that talk to graveside visitors with recorded messages amused him—almost as much as the Blue Limbo nonsense on everyone's tongues. It was, he understood fully, here and now that counted, not an extra few graceless weeks in some unfeeling wild blue yonder.

Bloody fools, he thought. All of them.

Taking the leather binder from the desk drawer, he wrote

two checks from the department's secret service fund account, set up to pay drug informers. One was for $14,000, the other for $8,000.

He sat back. They were the fifty-second and fifty-third checks he had written this year.

Galecki liked his autonomy. The checks didn't have to be countersigned.

There were no drug informers this week. In fact, there were rarely any.

The man in the black Buick watched Mitch Helwig leave his Pape Avenue apartment at eight o'clock the next morning and noted the time in his book. He did not bother to follow him this time. He had listened to the phone call between Helwig and his wife and knew that he was going to pick up his daughter for the weekend.

When Helwig's Chev disappeared onto Dundas Street, the man got out of the Buick and walked down to the corner of Queen. He had seen an all-night doughnut store there and wanted a sugar and caffeine hit.

His replacement, he knew, would be here by nine.

15 Karoulis, thought Mitch as he drove north on Greenwood across the Danforth, was right. Barbie was the key to his sanity, his balance. He should have begun setting up extended time with her before this.

Easier said than done.

The madness, the loss.

Leaving had been strewn with volcanic eruptions.

The black hole of memory... His mind tumbled into the vortex as he drove.

He remembered the morning after he had awakened stiff and cold on the grass beside his mother's grave, the morning after he had wreaked his havoc in the parking lot. The madness had still been simmering. It had bubbled delicately but steadily, like water at low heat on a back burner. As his head filled with images of Elaine and Donald Barbour together, he gave in to the adrenaline that pumped through his brain, pulled himself up from the damp ground, and strode unsteadily toward the fence, back to where he had left his car.

His blood had led him with an eerie clarity.

There had been more to do.

By eight A.M., he had parked opposite the Edenbridge Drive home in Etobicoke. He watched in silence as the two Barbour teenagers left for school.

A half hour later, the woman he took to be Ruth Barbour also left the house. Sitting in his Chev, Mitch placed the shotgun directional mike on the dashboard, still trained on the house. Nothing out of the ordinary had occurred in the conversations that he had monitored since arriving. Breakfast chitchat. What to thaw for dinner.

He watched the woman back the late-model Olds out of the driveway, watched it dwindle down the street toward the Kingsway, knowing from what he had heard that she was off to work for the day.

Mitch waited patiently. Listening.

At ten, the phone rang, startling Mitch from his torpor. He lifted the mike from the dashboard and trained it more accurately on the house, zeroing in on the source.

"Hello."

"It's me." Elaine's voice. *"Put on the video."*

"What happened?"

"He didn't come home last night. I don't know where he is."

"Have you changed your mind? About telling the police that you think it was him?"

"No."

"He's dangerous. You have to tell them."

"What did you tell Ruth?"

"That some nut was destroying cars in the parking lot while I ate dinner. That mine was one of them."

"What did she say?"

"Nothing much. Something about crime and violence getting out

of hand nowadays. Told her insurance covered everything, that it was all going to be little more than a giant nuisance."

"I'm scared. I don't know what to do."

A pause.

"Come over here."

"To your house?"

"Yes."

Mitch stiffened, listening.

"What about Ruth?"

"Everybody's gone for the day."

"I don't know." Mitch could hear the honest uncertainty in her voice.

"You'll be safe here, with me. He's dangerous. You shouldn't be alone."

Another pause. Then: *"How do I get there?"*

"Take a cab. I'll pay."

She sighed. *"I'll pay."*

"It doesn't matter. Just come."

Another sigh. Hesitation. *"All right."*

"Good. See you shortly."

Mitch heard the clicks as the connections broke. He stared at the house where his wife was headed, wondering how all this had happened, wondering at his own feelings. Both he and Elaine had gone their separate ways without consciously realizing it, and he was surprised at how little remorse he felt for the demise of the relationship itself. What did surprise him was the anger that he felt for this man who had intruded, who, he understood clearly, with his own masculine instincts and experience, did not love Elaine, but only loved himself, his successful life, his power.

Mitch took off the headphones and placed them and the mike on the seat beside him. Picking up the duffle bag from the floor of the passenger side, he stepped out of the car and closed the door behind him.

He glanced up at the sky. It looked like rain.

Mitch walked down the interlocking brick by the side of the house and into the backyard. At the rear of the house, sliding glass doors opened out onto a cedar deck. He reached into the duffel bag and took out a small Bausch & Lomb hand-laser as he mounted the steps toward the doors.

Placing the duffle bag at his feet, he trained the laser on the glass by the latch and slowly squeezed the trigger. It bubbled, sizzled, and cracked as he melted a swath big enough to permit his hand to reach through and open the lock.

He found himself standing in the kitchen, staring at the room where this man ate meals with his family: pine table, oak-trimmed cupboards, recessed lighting, and every conceivable technical gadget. This was a family that expected the best. Donald Barbour was a man who was used to getting what he wanted, accustomed to satisfying his appetites with ease and surety.

His eyes were drawn to the clear, crystal vase in the center of the table, with the freshly cut display of carnations, daisies, and wildflowers.

Mitch's anger focused, like the cobalt needle of laser that had just leaped from his fist, onto this man who lived so much better than he did, this man who had interfered in other people's lives, who would continue to do so long after Mitch had ceased intruding into his carefully contrived comfort zone.

But I'll see that he never forgets, Mitch thought. I'll explain that there's always a price to pay.

His hand tightened on the Bausch & Lomb and he listened intently. There was music coming from the second floor. A radio.

Mitch's movements became more precise. He placed the duffel bag on the pine table, opened it, and exchanged the hand-laser for the larger Sanyo with the folding shoulder-stock. It was far more powerful, and far more frightening to behold. Mitch wanted both effects.

With the bag in his left hand and the Sanyo buttressed in his right hand against his shoulder, he headed up the stairs.

The music grew louder. Mitch could hear movements from one of the rooms down the hall.

He followed the sounds.

The door was slightly ajar. Mitch eased it the rest of the way open with the barrel of the rifle.

It was the master bedroom, and Donald Barbour was primping the pillows at the head of the bed, oblivious to the intruder's presence. Mitch Helwig took in the room at a glance. He heard the soft music playing on the CD player in the corner and saw the two wine glasses marshaled beside the bottle chilling in the ice bucket.

He felt a wave of white-hot anger sweep over him, steeling his purpose and resolve.

"You were right." The words were spoken quietly.

Don Barbour snapped upright and turned around.

"I am dangerous."

The man's eyes widened in horror and disbelief as he absorbed the stranger, the weapon, the situation.

"You're a pig, Barbour. I just might roast you like a pig." He shifted the duffel bag to his left shoulder so that he could wield the Sanyo with both hands. Then he aimed it steadily at the ice bucket beside the bed and squeezed the trigger. It cracked vertically, then horizontally, as he moved the beam in a cross-motion, spilling water and ice cubes onto the broadloom. The bottle, under pressure, exploded, spraying glass and foaming liquid onto the wall behind it.

Don Barbour watched, stunned at the display of power and controlled violence. His face blanched visibly.

In the sudden silence that ensued, the two men faced one another.

"You're Mitch, right?" He licked his lips.

Mitch said nothing.

"You're making a mistake, Mitch. Nothing's happening. Nothing's going on."

Mitch shook his head. "I'm not making a mistake. You
are."

"For God's sake. You've got it all wrong."

He shook his head again. "No, I haven't. I finally understand." His eyes swept across the room.

This time Don Barbour said nothing in reply.

"I finally understand what I have to do."

"Jesus. Put that thing away." He gestured toward the rifle.
"You'll hurt somebody. There's been enough damage, enough
trouble." He was breathing excitedly now.

"You interfered in my life."

Barbour's eyes were frantic. "Christ almighty, man, you
neglected part of your life, ignored it."

Mitch's control shook apart with a seismic tremor, and the
rage in his brain exploded into reds and whites. "You fucking
pig." The skin of his face was pulled taut. His voice had
dropped in volume.

Barbour watched him, finally, truly frightened at what he
was confronting.

"You dare to tell me what I've ignored or neglected. You,
with your own wife and children, your own deceit and self-
indulgence, stand there like the puke that you are and dare to
censure me." In a sudden uncontrollable gesture, he kicked out
at the foot of the bed as hard as he could, venting the urge to
hurt this man, the need to dispel some of his fury physically.

The comforter on the bed undulated like the sea in response to his kick, and Mitch realized that he was standing beside a water bed. He realized that this was where this man had
hoped to take Elaine, and as earlier, the image of the two of
them together trickled into his rage-filled brain, and he acted
purely on a primal instinct.

He trained the Sanyo on the bed's water-filled mattress,
pressed the trigger, and zigzagged the barrel back and forth.
The water sluiced out.

"Jesus!" Donald Barbour's mouth hung open.

He cut the wooden frame and a ton of water poured

around their feet, across the floor, crashed against the walls, found the opening into the hall, and drained outward and toward the stairs.

Both men stood frozen.

Barbour put his hand to his forehead, speechless.

"You spoiled my day, I spoiled yours." Mitch looked at the pitiful figure before him, lowered his rifle and continued to stare at him. Finally, he turned and headed to the bedroom door. Turning, he studied the face of the man standing motionless against the wall, saw the look of bewilderment and fear etched there. "Going to be tough explaining it to your wife and children, isn't it?"

Don Barbour just stared at him, overcome.

Mitch turned and left the room.

He stopped momentarily in the kitchen on his way through, to reflect on its opulence. Success, he saw, as he had seen before, like self-professed virtue, was always a lie.

He swung the barrel of the Sanyo viciously through the crystal vase on the table as he strode out the door, shattering it, spraying water and flowers wildly in every direction.

The rain had begun as he got into his car and drove away.

16

Barbie had been up and ready for an hour. In her room, she had idled away some time reading *Nancy Drew and the Clue in the Ultrasonic Transformer*. Nancy was easy to identify with, since they both had fathers who were detectives or policemen. She knew her daddy worked hard and sometimes caught criminals too—although it probably wasn't as exciting as what she was reading.

Then she had killed some time drawing a picture—copying a funny face from her *Mad* magazine—using the special, French charcoal set that he had given her for Christmas.

Now she had just settled down on the floor to read the magazine and study the pictures for the hundredth time. She liked the Toys "R" U fake catalogue section: *Junior Tattoo Set; Fisher-Pricey Quicksand Box (Just Add Water); Unintendo Game Cartridges (50 titles to choose from! All basically the same game. Ages 8 to Death)*. The last one made her smile because it was the same kind of thing that her dad had always maintained was the case; he could never see the differences, no matter how many times she tried to explain them to him.

Her daddy had a new place to live—by himself. She worried about him. Who was going to take care of him? Would he have to eat all by himself? Wouldn't he get lonely?

Neither Daddy nor Mommy had been the same for a long time. They just weren't getting along is what her mom had told her. And she didn't know what she could do to help. Lots of kids she knew lived only with their mother. Jenny, who sat behind her in class, went every weekend up north to a place called Barrie and stayed there with her dad. He brought her back to her apartment on Sunday nights. There were two others that she knew in her class that lived only with their father. It wasn't that big a deal. But she had always thought that it would never happen to her. It did make her a bit sad. She didn't understand what had happened to make him want to leave, but it must have been pretty serious. Mommy was still angry a lot and didn't talk to her as much as she used to.

She lay back on the rug and stared at the ceiling. She missed him. He was funny. Going to see his new place would be great. It was like an adventure.

I guess, she thought, I'll have to take care of him.

Mommy doesn't think I should be reading *Mad* magazine. She says it'll make me too *cynical*—that's the word."

"I read *Mad* magazine when I was a kid."

"She mentioned that." Barbie looked out the window as they drove along.

There had been no incident, nothing but clinical courtesy on both sides as their daughter had been transferred into his care at the apartment.

"It'll teach you irony. It'll keep you from letting the world con you. Help you to see through things."

He glanced at her and saw what he perceived to be a rather wry smile on a nine-year-old. "Don't you think so?"

"I think she's afraid I'll be too much like you."

He smiled. "Wouldn't want that, would we?"

How's your work? Anything exciting to tell me?"

Mitch listened to the mock-adult conversation coming from his daughter. Her legs barely hung over the edge of the seat, he saw, stealing a quick appraisal of her tiny form as they continued down Greenwood.

He mulled over what to tell her, decided on an anecdote that would suffice. "We cut down speeding on the Don Valley Parkway by putting a mannequin—a store dummy—named 'Officer Gregory' in a police skimmer by the side of the road. Now we got a kidnapping case. Somebody stole Gregory."

She giggled.

"We've sent out an APB: legless mannequin, weight five kilograms, dressed like a cop, a bit thick, no known personal problems, and works cheap. Unarmed."

She was still giggling.

"In the big city," he said, "things just go from bad to worse."

"This is neat." Barbie dragged her bag up the stairs behind her. "It's like a secret place to live. Neat," she said again.

"It is kind of neat, now that you mention it." Reaching the third landing, he pulled out his key and opened the door, swinging it inward. He watched her face. "Well?"

She was mesmerized, staring within.

"What do you think?"

She went inside, eyed the sloped ceilings, his newly acquired table and chairs. She put her bag down and zipped to give the washroom a quick appraisal, then went into the living area and gazed up at the skylight.

"I open that to chase the pigeons off the roof. Their cooing drives me crazy."

Barbie's eyes spotted the golden bust positioned on the floor in the corner of the living area. "What's that?"

"That's a piece of art I purchased. Give the place some class. What do you think?"

"Who is it?"

"It's Elvis."

Her eyes widened.

"You heard of him?"

She nodded. "His picture's on the front of the newspapers where Mommy shops for groceries, lots of times. He's a ghost or something."

Mitch nodded. "Or something."

Her eyes darted around. "Where do I sleep?"

"In here." He pointed to one of the two rooms to the left of the entrance hall. "I put this door on yesterday. Found it in the basement. Somebody removed all the doors in here, to open up the place. But you need some privacy. Right?"

"Don't you have a door for your bedroom?"

"There were two others in the basement. I can get one if I want." He thought for a minute. "Maybe I should. Later."

She looked inside the room, saw the mattress with the purple stain on the floor, the blankets beside it. Then she looked at her father.

He smiled, shrugged his shoulders.

She shrugged and smiled back.

What are we going to do today?"

"What do you usually do on Saturday?"

"Watch TV. Go shopping with Mommy." She made a face.

"I haven't got a TV yet. But we gotta do some shopping."

She started to make the face again.

"I need your help. You have to give me the benefit of your experience, help me buy some food, other things."

She considered this. "Okay. What else?"

"Maybe catch a movie later today."

She was still considering it all.

"Maybe fix up your room. Make it so you'll be comfortable here. Right?"

"Can I get a desk to draw on? Do my homework on?"

"You got it, beautiful. It'll be our project for the weekend."

"Good." She tossed her bag into her room.

After shopping, with the trunk full of groceries, Mitch headed to the Chinese and Vietnamese market area at Broadview and Gerrard.

He pulled to the side of the road and activated the parking flashers. "Wait here," he said.

The sidewalks were thronged. Barbie watched out the window as he went across the street to talk to a man wearing a white apron, selling fruit and vegetables from wooden stands outside his store. The man nodded, waved his hand toward a pile of wooden crates. Mitch picked up three of them and crossed back over to the car, put them in the backseat.

"What are they for?" she asked.

"Furniture." He smiled. "One of them can be a chair for your desk. The other two can be piled on top of one another for a place to keep your things."

"Neat," she said.

He started the car, cut into the traffic, and made a left at Broadview.

When he pulled over in front of a construction site on Dundas, Barbie's interest perked up again. "What now?"

"See those cement blocks?"

She followed his pointing finger with her eyes. "Yes."

"Four of them should do." He got out of the car, opened the rear door on his side, and came back a minute later with a concrete building block which he placed carefully on the floor of the backseat. He did this three more times.

Barbie watched in amazement. Finally, she asked: "Isn't this stealing?"

Mitch shrugged. "If they knew that I needed them for a

beautiful, bright little girl like you, they'd donate them without blinking an eye." He smiled. "I believe that. I really do."

He started the car and they headed off.

It took them twenty minutes to haul groceries, wooden fruit crates, and cement blocks to the third floor, and when they were done, Mitch sat on the floor with the sweat pouring down his face. Barbie sat down beside him, not nearly as tired, since he had clearly borne the brunt of the labor.

"What now?" she asked.

"Well," he said, "when my heart stops pounding, our next trip is to the basement."

Mitch lugged the two doors up the winding stairway, one at a time, with Barbie hanging onto the bottom end in a token way in each case. The first he attached to the doorway of what was his bedroom. Then he piled the cement blocks in two sets of two a little more than a meter apart in Barbie's room and laid the other door flat across them, the doorknob jutting up on the side near the wall.

"There," he said.

Her eyes were wide.

"It's your desk." He placed a wooden fruit crate in front of it, turning it on its side, as a seat.

Barbie sat down on the crate. Her knees fit just beneath the horizontal door. Then she beamed up at him, her eyes alive. "It's wonderful," she said.

He sat down on the floor beside her.

"Wonderful," she said again.

And it was.

They sat at the gray plastic table eating their homemade hamburgers and drinking milk.

"Not bad," she said. "Not bad at all."

He nodded agreement. "My first home-cooked meal." Then: "How's your mom doing?"

"Okay." She continued chewing.

Mitch tried another conversational gambit. "How's Lottie?" he asked, referring to her best friend.

"She's fine. Her brother broke his nose, though."

"He did? How?"

She giggled. "He cooked a golf ball in the microwave oven and it exploded. Broke his nose."

"What?"

"He put it in the microwave and cooked it to see what would happen. Pretty dumb. But he's only seven, you know. Then he took it out and about ten seconds later it blew up. Sprayed liquid rubber all over his mother's kitchen and broke his nose." She giggled again. "It's ridiculous, isn't it?"

Mitch looked flabbergasted.

"He's just a dumb kid. His parents were mad, but glad he's okay." She paused to drink some milk. "Kids," she said. "Some of them will do anything to see what happens."

"You're too mature for that kind of stuff, right?"

"Right."

"Tell you what. You want to know something, you ask me, okay? I'll tell you. No need to experiment. Is he okay now?"

"He's fine. Got a stupid bandage on his nose, though." She couldn't stop giggling. "It's funny."

Mitch giggled a bit too.

She was chewing her hamburger, thinking. "I can ask you anything I want to know?"

Mitch looked at her.

"Can I?"

He nodded. "That's what I said."

"I'm nine now. You told me when I was nine, you'd tell me where babies came from."

Mitch chewed for a moment himself, thinking. "I said that?"

She nodded. "Yup."

"When?"

"When I was six."

"Your mother hasn't explained it to you?"

"Some of it."

Mitch tried to remember how old he had been when he had uncovered the facts of life. He recalled vividly how John Lovasz, a kid in third grade, had explained it to a group of them in the school yard and how shocked he had been. It had explained much that he had wondered about, including how Monica McClonsky, the sixteen-year-old who lived down the street from them, had been able to have a baby without being married. His mother had told him when he asked that she had just gone out with boys too much until her system didn't know the difference. That had been a whole new idea to him. He also remembered, after John had made things clear, not quite being able to believe that his parents could ever do such a thing.

Mitch thought it would be nice to be able to tell it straight, not like his mother had done, and definitely not with the images that John Lovasz had employed. It felt as if the mantle of parenthood had descended on him fully, and he was determined to accept it, to do a good job.

"When do you want to talk about it?"

"Now." Her big bright eyes stared at him, waiting. She took another bite of her burger and chewed.

He cleared his throat, thinking.

"What part do you want to hear?"

"All of it."

Mitch rubbed the side of his neck. "Right. All of it." He hesitated. "You know that babies grow inside the mother's stomach for nine months, then they get born because they're too big to stay in there any longer, and after nine months they're fully formed little people." He looked at her. "You know that?"

She nodded. "You told me that before. Mommy told me too."

"What do you want to know then?"

"How do they get in the mother's stomach? I still don't get it."

Mitch smiled, closed his eyes, tried to picture his own father ever having this conversation with him, and knew that it had not happened because it never could have happened. He would never have dreamed of approaching his father at Barbie's age, and his father would have been totally unprepared.

Like I'm totally unprepared.

It's happening, he thought. A watershed moment. I've got to do it right. I want to do it right.

He opened his eyes.

She was waiting.

"The man has a penis and the woman has a vagina. You know this, don't you?"

"Yes."

"Well, when a man loves and cares for a woman, and they make a mutual decision to have a baby and raise that baby, it's normal for the man's penis to become stiff and swollen. It's natural and healthy."

"Like Horace."

"Pardon?"

"Jenny's dog. That happened to him. They had to get him fixed."

A momentary derailment. "Yes. Like Jenny's dog. It's normal and healthy for it to happen to all male animals." He continued. "He can then, if they both agree, insert his penis into the woman's vagina. Nature has a way of allowing the woman's vagina to lubricate in order to more easily accept the man's penis at the moment of this decision."

He watched her face. She was rapt.

"You know the F-word that people use when they're angry or frustrated?"

She nodded.

"That's really the word that describes this action. It's also called sexual intercourse."

Her eyes were unblinking.

I'm doing it, he thought. I think I'm doing okay. Tell it straight. Do it right.

"Then the man oozes a liquid into the woman. It contains sperm—"

"Sounds like a whale."

A bemused smile crept onto his face. "I guess it does. Anyway, this sperm fertilizes the egg that the woman has, and the baby begins to grow."

Tasteful, he thought. And careful, and accurate. And discreet. He had given her the truth the way that he had never gotten it. It wouldn't do to mention that perhaps "oozes" wasn't exactly the most accurate verb for how the liquid usually transferred, but he thought that "pounded out like a jackhammer" might scare her unduly.

He sat back, proud of himself.

"How does the liquid ooze out of the man?"

He frowned. "What do you mean?"

"Does he throw up on her or what?"

Mitch was speechless.

She waited.

And he thought he had done so well. Who can guess the mysteries of life from a kid's point of view?

"It comes out of his penis when it's inside the woman's vagina," he explained evenly.

Barbie looked momentarily stunned. This was the part that she had been missing. She took a long swig of her milk, then said, "I get it now."

Mitch smiled, relieved.

"What're we going to do after dinner?" She was ready for a new topic.

"How about a movie?"

"I never go to movies at night."

"This'll be a first. There's going to be a lot of firsts from now on. Right?"

"Right." She wiped the milk mustache from her upper lip with the back of her hand.

"Let's see if we can find a funny movie."

She smiled. "Okay." With her legs swinging back and forth, she turned her attention to the golden bust in the corner of the room. "Is he dead or alive?"

Mitch followed her gaze, considered. "A bit of both," he said.

She looked puzzled.

"A bit of both," he repeated.

Barbie studied her father's face to see if she was being kidded.

She couldn't tell.

When Mitch entered the elevator with Barbie to return her to her mother's apartment Sunday night, he felt better than he had in months. There'd been the movie last night—a comedy—cooking the bacon and eggs with her this morning, lunch at McDonald's, the new *Mad* magazine and drawing paper and pencils they'd picked up at the World's Biggest Book Store downtown, and the casserole fiasco that was dinner.

It had all been good.

He looked at her standing in front of him, her head tipped back as she watched the light move through the numbers over the doors.

Elaine was waiting outside the apartment door in the hall when they stepped out of the elevator. Barbie smiled at her and waved, but took his hand. He squeezed it.

When they were within two meters of the doorway, Mitch bent and kissed and hugged her. She hugged him back.

Elaine watched.

Mitch stood up. "I'd like to pick her up Wednesday after school, take her back to school the next morning, then pick her up next Friday for the weekend, if you've got no other plans."

Elaine's eyes narrowed.

Barbie reached up to take his hand. Then she spoke. "Can I Mommy? Please. It'd be fun. Mrs. Chan's here on Wednesdays anyway."

Elaine Helwig dropped her eyes to her daughter. "We'll discuss it, dear. It's late now. You've got school tomorrow."

She went and took her mother's hand, turned and waved to her father. Mitch smiled as she went inside.

Elaine gave him an icy glare.

"I'll call you tomorrow," he said. "We'll discuss it." He turned and left. The weekend had been too good to spoil it now.

17

From the Thorncliffe apartment complex, Mitch went west, then south across the Leaside bridge, veered onto Pape, then turned west again at Mortimer heading for the Bayview extension. It was only eight o'clock — pretty early, he thought, to go back to his apartment and sit by himself.

I can see him now, he thought, sitting in that room glued to the goddamn TV. Or maybe I'm wrong. Maybe he's with Flo, dispensing theories and opinions like a gumball machine. Or maybe he's planning how to make his move on her — if he hasn't already.

The thought gave him hope, since right now he didn't feel like making a move on anybody.

He thought of Barbie, how good she was for him. Karoulis had been right. He was already looking forward to Wednesday.

Kids, he thought. He'd always figured that you had to save them from all the crap of the world, all the pain. And it was true. You did. But what he hadn't realized until this weekend was how it was such a two-way street. It was them who helped save you from the crap and pain of the world.

Fascinating. They were a doubly valuable resource.

He recalled the article that had appeared in the *Toronto Sun* last month about bulletproof back-to-school clothing that was being touted as the latest fashion rage. There'd been a raft of killings of children on the streets in the last year from stray bullets, and the media had seized upon it. Some guy had seen an angle, had started his own company called My Bodyguard. You could outfit your kid in a jacket made of Kevlar—bullet-proof denim-colored, smart, sporty—weight about a kilo, all for a mere two hundred and fifty bucks. The guy claimed to have received about a thousand calls as soon as the product was announced.

And what about lasers? Weren't the kids' vests already obsolete? He thought of the Silent Guard that he had bought last year for just that reason.

Mitch didn't know. It sounded crazy.

But then, nearly everything else sounded crazy too.

Mitch pulled over at a parking meter on Davenport west of Yonge. He had been watching the headlights in his rearview mirror since he had turned off the Bayview extension onto Rosedale Valley Road. They had remained constant three or four vehicles behind him the whole way. He sat in the car and waited for the other vehicle to pass him, hoping to get a look at it and the driver, maybe a license number. But the car had slowed on Yonge when he had turned right onto Davenport and had not followed. Twisting his head about, he saw only that the car that continued south on Yonge was a large, black American vehicle.

His senses heightened and his skin prickled.

Karoulis. Huziak.

Evans. Lim.

The names rang in his head.

He realized where he had just been, where he was headed, and didn't like the idea that anyone might know this much about him.

The king of England earns five million a day in interest payments alone. And he pays no taxes. Can you fuckin' believe it?" Paul Helwig bristled as Mitch sat down in the chair opposite him. "He's got crown assets and private income. Crown assets, he can't sell. Private income . . . " He let the scorn drip from the phrase. "Ridiculous. I suppose he earned it in his private life. Maybe doing a private job. What kind of private job can you get if you live in Buckingham Palace? I know. He cuts hair as a sideline. His staff's hair. That's it."

He was fun to watch when he was on a roll, Mitch thought.

"How you doing?"

"Good," Mitch said.

"You eatin' okay?"

Mitch nodded. "Doing good. Had Barbie for the weekend. Just took her back to her mother. Forced me to live like a human being for a couple of days. Got my head screwed on straight for the first time in a long while. Had fun."

"Good." He reached over to the end table beside his bed and held up a small newspaper. "Everybody here gets this thing."

"What is it?"

"Called *Especially for Seniors*. We get it every two months. Half of us haven't got eyes good enough to read it. Which reminds me—the CNIB—the Institute for the Blind—sends out its own newsletter to members too. Figure that one out. Anyway, Flo reads some of this to me when it comes. Look at the article on the front page."

Mitch reached over and took it from him. The article was titled "Canada's Seniors Blamed for Financial Problems." Mitch raised his eyebrows.

"Some snot-nose University of Toronto professor figures that escalating health-care costs and dwindling pension reserves are our fault." Paul Helwig frowned angrily. "We're living too long. Not productive enough."

"Wonder if he's got a mother or father?"

"He hasn't got a dick or balls either, let alone any fuckin' brains. Professor, my bare ass. Wait'll he gets to be eighty-four and has to listen to the assholes of the world—guys like him. Smart guys. Guys who make speeches."

Mitch shrugged. "You said it yourself. He's an asshole. The world's full of them. Forget him." He tossed the paper onto the bed.

"Why don't they put in that paper something inspiring? Something positive? There's another piece in there from the *New England Journal of Medicine.* You get old. You may lose your teeth. You may lose your hair. And according to this other guy, if you're a man, you may lose a big chunk of your brain tissue."

"What are you talking about?"

"They did autopsies of sixty-two brains. Found that as men age the size of their corpus callosum gets smaller. Language and speech are affected. Female sex hormones may protect women's brains from the same kind of atrophy, it says."

Mitch didn't know exactly what to say.

"Especially for Seniors," he sneered. "Why don't they just send us color brochures of funeral homes and arrangements?"

"Get Flo to write a letter to the editor. Get everybody in the building to sign it. Tell them that if they don't print something useful and positive, you'll have thousands of seniors send their paper back to them with no postage on it, and they'll have to pay the postage due. Show them some senior power."

His father looked at him, surprised. "Why didn't I think of that? It's brilliant." He smiled. "Maybe my brain is shrinking."

"As long as that's all that's shrinking."

The old man continued looking at him, his smile growing more wily. "TV news had an item last week about a ninety-two-year-old Australian farmer and docker who had just become a father."

Mitch's eyebrows went up.

"His wife, a Fiji Indian, was thirty-eight. Said her husband was 'real strong.' They don't plan any more kids, because she says she's too old."

"Ninety-two. Jesus. Must be a record."

"Guinness only lists the oldest mothers. There's no record of oldest fathers." He adopted a self-satisfied expression and sat back smugly. "So," he said emphatically, "it's just my fuckin' brain that's shrinking. That's all."

Watched *Eye on Toronto* Friday mornin'. They did a feature on that Spiricom machine we saw on the Zwolinski show. Remember?"

"The Blue Limbo business? I remember."

"Sunnybrook Hospital's got one. They were interviewing people there about it." The old man scratched his jaw. "Said they were just getting it operational."

Sunnybrook, Mitch realized, was where his father's doctors were. He saw an opthamologist there, a skin specialist, and somebody else, Mitch recalled. Clearly, it had given the senior Helwig a lot to think about that was not just philosophical or theoretical; it was all pretty close to home.

"The brain," Paul Helwig said. "Shrinking. Not shrinking. Living after the body dies. Makin' a guy's dick hard at age ninety-two. Who can figure it?'

Mitch chuckled.

"People who live in the Soviet Arctic are mostly left-handed. Only a quarter of them are right-handed."

"How do you know?" Mitch asked.

"Saw it on *Unsolved Mysteries.* That's weird enough, but what they really can't explain is why the righties age faster in the extreme cold than the southpaws."

Mitch didn't know what to say.

"See what I mean?"

"No."

"The brain. Nobody can fuckin' figure it."

"I think it's yours that nobody can figure, Dad."

The old man ignored this. "Guy in North Carolina woke up back in 1991 after being in a coma—what was described as a vegetative state—for eight years." He looked at Mitch. "Eight *years.* He'd been clubbed on the head with a log in 1982. Asked for his favorite foods and said he wanted to walk again."

"Was this on TV too?"

"Unexplained Phenomena. Was a rerun. Everything's a rerun. Tuesdays at nine. CTV. They showed a film of the guy. He looked awful. Emaciated. You know."

"I can imagine."

"Another guy in Baltimore began speaking with a Scandinavian accent after suffering a stroke."

"Dad?"

"Hmm?"

"Nobody's got a more fascinating brain than you have."

The old man smiled. "The stuff I think of."

"I'll bet."

"It'd scare you."

Mitch nodded, smiling.

The old man pointed at his son. "And you should've paid more attention to me before it shrunk by twenty percent."

Mitch leaned back laughing softly and put his hands behind his head. I'll bet, he thought. I'll bet.

Bring Barbie over for a visit next time you can. I don't see her enough." Paul Helwig scratched at his chin.

"I will. Good idea. She needs some of your wisdom."

"You bet she does. You all do."

A knock at the door surprised him. Mitch looked at his father.

"Probably Flo," the old man said. "I was expecting her."

The image of a ninety-two-year-old Australian and a Fiji Indian woman flashed into Mitch's head. "Hope I'm not interfering."

"Course not. We were goin' to watch some TV. Shoot the breeze."

"I'll get it," Mitch said, rising and walking to the door.

Flo looked surprised when she realized that it was not Paul who was in front of her. "Mitch," she said as recognition dawned. She touched him gently at the elbow. "How's your shoulder?"

"Great, Flo. Thanks to you."

She smiled at his kindness.

"Tell her to c'mon in. Don't block the door. How many visitors do you think I get? You think I can afford to make 'em wait in the hall?"

Mitch stepped aside, placed his hand behind her shoulders and escorted her inside. "Sit down, Flo." He indicated the chair where he had been sitting, and sat himself down on the edge of the bed.

Paul Helwig nodded, approving of the etiquette. "You know the kind of visitors I get? Church of Latter-Day Saints. Seventh Day Adventists. They get in the building somehow. Gonna save us old people. Ministers. Nuns. They come and want to know if you'd like visitors, want to make sure you're not lonely. Then they produce a Bible or prayer book and try to leave it with you. Had a guy knock on my door last week. When I open it, I see this youngster, shirt and tie, barely shavin', standin' there, askin' me if he can talk about the Lord with me. I told him he was wet behind the ears. Told him I'd forgotten more religion than he ever knew. Told him to take his tie off and go find a woman and quit botherin' other people."

Flo laughed.

"I was right. But he won't listen. Guys like that are stone dumb. You can't dent 'em." He looked at his son. "You and Elaine finished?"

Mitch didn't answer immediately, turning to glance at Flo instead.

"I talked to Flo about it," his father said.

"Oh." A pause. "In that case, the answer is yes."

"You need to take your tie off and find a woman too, then."

"I don't wear a tie."

The old man shrugged. "Depends."

Mitch nodded. "Right. It does." He paused. "It's a little soon, that's all."

His father considered this. "Maybe."

"I have a son and two daughters," Flo said. "Both my daughters have been through divorces. Paul and I talked about everything involved after you left last time. It was good for both of us."

Mitch relaxed. The trouble that you could get into in your head was thinking that things had only happened to you.

"Love. Sex. Marriage . . ." Paul Helwig trailed off. "It all goes back to the brain, and who can figure it?"

"The brain?" Mitch asked.

"How we see things. What we think. Decisions we think we're making."

Mitch thought of it more like an airplane that was going down, and no matter how much you worked and fiddled with the controls, it was going down anyway. Best you could do was bail out with as many others as possible.

He thought of Barbie.

"Tell him about kisses," Flo said.

Mitch looked at her in surprise. "Has he got you going now?"

"We listened to it on the Sandy Zwolinski show. It was very interesting."

"Guy wrote an article in the *British Journal of Dermatology*—"

"Jesus, Dad—"

"Hey! Give me a chance. Don't be so skeptical." He looked at Flo. "Right, Flo?"

"Right. It was very interesting."

"So," his father pressed on, only slightly deterred, "the guy says that love's only a chemical reaction and kissing's just the way folks imbibe the needed drug. He says we sample the semiochemicals of the other person when we kiss, get a kind of biological signal, one animal to another. Say these chemi-

cals come out of the sebaceous glands—a substance called
sebum. These glands are all over the body—lots of 'em in the
mouth, on the borders of the lips, scalp, face, neck—all around
the female nipples too—excuse me, Flo . . ."

"That's all right. It's what he said."

"So, like I said, it all goes back to the brain. And maybe
you and Elaine stopped reacting chemically. Wrong chemicals.
What do you think?"

Mitch almost laughed. "You could be right. Who knows?"

"Must happen all the time. Explains lots."

Mitch looked at Flo. "Do you believe it?"

"Makes sense to me."

Paul Helwig looked pleased.

"But," she continued, "it's probably a lot more compli-
cated than that too. There are so many other factors. Don't you
think so too, Paul?"

The old man eyed her shrewdly, gauging his answer.
"Probably," he said. Then he smiled.

Mitch watched her smile in return. *Kissin's just the way folks
imbibe the needed drug.* Christ, he thought, watching the two of
them eyeing each other like kids.

How I need that drug.

THREE

. . . a sail drew near, nearer, and picked me up at last. It was the devious cruising Rachel, that in her retracing search after her missing children, only found another orphan.

—Herman Melville
Moby Dick

18

"Burglars hit a Metro home every twenty minutes, Huziak."

It was nine A.M., Monday.

"Those are the ones that are reported."

"I know, Captain."

"Twenty-four hours a day. Seven days a week."

"I know, Captain." He placed Karoulis's Styrofoam cup of coffee in front of him, trying to avoid the piles of uneven papers arrayed on the desk.

"We finally topped the three hundred and fifty thousand mark last year in total criminal code offenses in the city. A new record. The newspapers find it almost as interesting as the number of people who watch the Jays each season at the Dome." He pushed the morning copy of the *Sun* aside.

"It's a little hot."

"What?"

"The coffee. Be careful."

"Oh. Thanks."

"The numbers are fascinating, aren't they?"

"You could say that. Fascinating is one way of putting it." Karoulis tried his coffee, found that it was hot, set it back down.

"Homicide boys had some numbers out of Washington they were tossing around last week. Trying to make themselves feel better," Huziak said. "U.S. Senate judiciary staff reported that forty-two thousand people will be murdered in the States this year. Somebody kills somebody every twelve minutes. How're those for numbers that're fascinating? That's a small city—wiped out."

"Jesus."

"We're not in that league, yet."

"This is a big city. We're gettin' there." Karoulis looked at the staff sergeant. "You heard about Louise?"

Huziak looked puzzled. "Who?"

"Louise. The pig."

Huziak didn't seem to follow the thread at all.

"Werner von Franke, in Narcotics, says he's pioneered a new crime-fighting weapon—Louise, the pig. Says she can outdo any dog in sniffing out narcotics, explosives, any other aromatic contraband—and can keep on working in intense heat long after police dogs have given up. Claims she's not easily distracted by other noises and smells, like dogs. Says she's very sensitive, but has nerves like steel wire."

"Louise, the pig," Huziak repeated.

"Von Franke says she holds the official rank of SWS— for *Schnuffelwildschwein.*"

"Okay," said Huziak, "I'll bite." He was seating himself opposite Karoulis with a file folder on his lap.

"Means 'sniffing wild boar.' "

"You're right, Captain."

Karoulis raised his eyebrows.

"It is a big city. We are getting there. Wherever there is."

Karoulis was eyeing the file folder. "What's on tap this morning? The stuff that the newspapers will like."

Huziak took a sheet from the folder, held it at arm's length. "Windshields of about two hundred vehicles were smashed in five underground parking lots on St. George Street. They've charged two males, aged sixteen and nineteen, nabbed near one of the garages. They were carrying baseball bats. Damage estimated at a hundred and fifty thousand dollars."

"Motive? Theft?"

"Kicks."

"Kicks," Karoulis repeated. "Right."

"Arrested three men and seeking two more," Huziak continued, "after a vehicle was stopped at four A.M. Sunday at Front and Market Streets. Guy bolted from the front passenger seat. Inside the car, they found what Browning of the Asian crime unit called a 'home invasion kit': a sawed-off .30–.30-caliber rifle, eight-mm ammunition, five General Electric handlasers, three sets of handcuffs, two machetes, two rubber masks, and nine Ninja masks. They subsequently searched one of their homes and seized a semiautomatic handgun fitted with a silencer, night-vision glasses, and a quantity of crack cocaine. One of the men, a Malaysian, is in custody with Canada Immigration."

Karoulis just nodded, listening.

"Oh, yeah—von Franke's going to give the press something solid about their eleven-month investigation with the RCMP, the OPP, and Customs and Immigration. They've arrested seven Metro residents. He figures they made a hundred million bucks, bringing about five hundred kilos of high-grade 'China White' heroin into North America in the past two years. Went from Hong Kong through Toronto to the U.S. market— particularly New York City. Seized nine-point-six million dollars in cash, more than a kilo of ninety-nine percent pure heroin, street value eight-point-two million dollars, ten sophisticated Israeli-made Uzi submachine guns, seven pistols— one fitted with a silencer—and four Mitsubishi laser rifles."

"Press will love it. Was SWS Louise involved?"

Huziak smiled. "Didn't ask."

"Would've been front page, then."

Huziak and Karoulis both paused to sip their coffees. Karoulis, aching for a cigarette, found himself turning a pen end over end in his left hand. "You ever been in therapy, Huziak?"

The question seemed to take the staff sergeant, who was used to his captain's non sequiturs, by surprise. "You mean, like psychological therapy?"

Karoulis nodded. "Yeah."

He shook his head. "Can't say that I have."

"Don't bother," Karoulis said. "Mostly bullshit." He paused, thinking. "I went for a couple of months after I broke up with my first wife. A lady psychologist. Thinking back, I figure she was as fucked up as anyone else." His eyes moved to the wall, fixing there. "We go to experts to explain our own lives to us, explain our children. We pay them. Tell us, we say, how to deal with our wives, our girlfriends, our mothers, our boss." He paused. "This one told me that most people had unsatisfactory sex lives, that I had to learn to appreciate the little things in life. She rose as she was talking and went to the window of the office and looked out. Talked about the birds and the flowers. She was very plain looking." Another pause. "I feel sorry for her now."

Huziak didn't say anything.

"She was fucking nuts," he said very gently, smiling at Huziak. "And I paid her. I was hoping she'd have the answer."

"You had to try."

Did you have Louise give this office the once-over?"

"Louise might be the answer," said Huziak.

Both of them recalled the Semtex, the explosion that had blown the two of them over like straws in a wind, that had killed Evans and Lim.

"I check it every morning myself, Captain. I don't want to get my ass blown off before I have my coffee."

"Maria's coming home from Montreal for a visit. I'd like to keep my ass intact for a while too."

"How's she doing?"

"Great. I think she's a fucking genius or something. Ph.D. work. Teaching assistant at McGill. Guess she got my genes." He smiled at Huziak.

"Yeah. Right. How's Helwig doing? He okay?"

Karoulis frowned. "Don't know. He's tough. Very tough. But a guy can only take so much, you know?"

Huziak nodded. "Ain't it the truth." He changed the topic.
"Galecki was apparently in on the weekend, talking to Polonich and some others, seeing if they had anything new on the explosion in your office."

"He was?"

"Yeah. Interestin', eh?"

"Very."

"What'd he find out?"

"Nothin'."

"Then?"

"Then he left. That's what Polonich said."

The information tickled Karoulis's brain like gossamer threads.

19

"You want to go *where?*"

"You heard me. Madagascar." Maria Karoulis stared at her father with a half-smile across the dinner table. She buttered a roll and arranged her napkin on her lap in the interval of his astonishment.

Helen Karoulis met her stepdaughter's eyes warmly and nodded enthusiasm for her declaration.

"I don't even know where the hell Madagascar is," announced Sam Karoulis leaning back in his chair, looking perplexed.

"It's a big island, off the east coast of Africa. The Malagasy Republic. It's one of the most unique places on the planet—yet one of the most representative, as a microcosm. It's the subject of my dissertation."

"How big an island?"

"Enormous. Bigger than the entire British Isles. Bigger than New Zealand. Bigger than Texas. And," she added the zinger, "much bigger than Greece."

Karoulis started at the mention of his birthplace.

Helen laughed.

He turned to his wife. "Do you understand this?"

"Of course. She's a big girl. Twenty-five years old. She's doing her dissertation on Madagascar. She wants to go there for some field study. Makes perfect sense to me. Pass the rolls, please."

A big girl. Madagascar. He couldn't adjust this quickly. She was still his little girl, always would be, and the thought of her on the other side of the world in some backward country filled him with anxiety. Living in Montreal these past few years had been bad enough.

"All right." He sat back, lifted his wineglass. "I'm listening. I'm trying to be a rational man, even though I'm your father, and the two concepts are mutually exclusive."

His eyes drank in the sight of his daughter, a young, dark-eyed beautiful woman now, transposing the image over the little girl of his memory.

"It's called the Great Red Island, because of the fertile red soil throughout the country—especially on the west coast. It drifted away from Africa a hundred and sixty-five million years ago. It was once covered with forest, but four-fifths of that forest is gone, and projections are that in twenty years there will be hardly any left at all. The land is being cleared primarily for agriculture, but shortly after it's cleared, the soil loses its nutrients and the cycle continues. People slash and burn to clear land to grow rice and to create pasture land for cattle. Forests are burned to produce charcoal, since most people are too poor to buy kerosene. When the trees go, the soil follows. It's the most eroded place on earth. It's a microcosm: rapid human population growth pits man against nature, putting unacceptable demands on the environment." She paused to eat and drink.

Both Helen and Sam listened intently.

"The rivers run red with the earth, and the whole country looks like it's bleeding, hemorrhaging. It's a metaphor for the planet."

"When would you go?" Helen asked.

"In the fall."

"For how long?" asked Sam.

"Don't know. Enough time to research and learn. Maybe see what can be done to divert the path to self-destruction. Then I'd come back and finish my dissertation."

"Sounds exciting," Helen said. "Can you afford it?"

"I can't afford anything. I get paid peanuts, and grant money is tight and limited. But I'll go anyway, somehow." She reflected between bites. "I taught two courses last year: Introduction to Physical Geography—atmospheric, biospheric and lithospheric systems and their interactions—and Biogeography—analysis of past and present plant and animal distributions, of environmental and biological constraints, impact of continental drift, quaternary climatic changes and human interference on contemporary patterns. It was the second course that got me interested in Madagascar, got me focused."

Sam Karoulis looked unconvinced. "I don't know," he mused. "There're a lot of weirdos out there. Might be dangerous for a woman in Madagascar."

"It's dangerous for a woman right here. And for a man," his daughter added emphatically.

"It's the policeman and the father in him combined," said Helen. "It's too much for him. Maybe on a full stomach. Maybe during dessert he might relax."

"We caught a guy last month, caught him red-handed," said Karoulis, "with a fishing rod, reeling in ladies' clothing from a washline. When they searched his apartment, they found hundreds of bras, slips, nighties, bathing suits, bikinis, dresses, slacks, shoes, boots. Like that. You name it."

Maria laughed.

"Weirdos," he said. "Probably weirdos in Madagascar too."

"Madagascar is magic," Maria said. "It's an alien world right in our midst. There's the indri, a lemur, the size of a tiny child, face of a stuffed bear, has a song like a whale. The aye-aye, creature of the night, black and silver, ears like a bat, teeth like a beaver, long skinny middle finger that locals believe brings death, but is actually used to dig insects out of soft wood. The rare golden bamboo lemur, only a few left, eats enough cyanide daily to kill a human being."

Sam and Helen Karoulis listened to their daughter tumble into the magic, beginning to understand, remembering when they themselves were subject to magic, softening.

"Two-thirds of the world's chameleons hide in Madagascar, changing colors with their moods. There are fish that leap from the rivers and climb tree trunks. Fat, round tenrecs, with spikes like a hedgehog, but yellow, waddle through the underbrush. Spiny trees, with octopuslike branches; thick baobab trees, with spongy wet interiors; a palm tree you can slice into and get drinkable, crystal water."

To Sam Karoulis, it didn't sound like the world that he knew or lived in. It did sound like a magic kingdom, maybe the right place for his little girl.

He smiled. "I'll help you get there," he said.

Maria beamed. "Thanks, Daddy."

Helen reached over and took his hand.

Parked on Glen Manor Drive, the man in the black Buick listened to the dinner conversation within the Karoulis household with indifference. When he discerned that they had finished their meal, he sat in the dark interior of his vehicle for several more hours, his patience controlled and uncanny. When, finally, his surveillance systems told him that both the females were on the second floor, and Karoulis himself was alone in the living room, he checked his watch.

11:10 P.M.

It was time.

The street was empty. There was no moon.

He turned the key, started the car, let the engine idle. Then he put his hand in his pocket, took out the tiny Sony hand-laser, palmed it, pulled his hat low on his face, and got out of the car. He walked up the steps, stood in front of the door, rang the bell, and waited.

When Sam Karoulis opened the door, he looked with great surprise into the man's face, then with incomprehension at the laser pointed at his chest.

The man squeezed the trigger gently. The needle of light made no sound as it pierced Karoulis's heart. The police captain's eyes still registered the same incomprehension as he fell backward against the closet door of his hallway and slid to the floor.

Within seconds, the black Buick pulled from the curb and turned into the traffic on Queen Street.

20

At 11:15 p.m., Mitch Helwig's phone rang. He left the newspaper that he was reading on the gray plastic table, picked up the receiver and activated the video.

Helen Karoulis's panic-filled, almost hysterical face filled the screen. "Mitch! You're the closest. I didn't know who else to call. Sam's been shot. He might be dead. I called an ambulance already."

A whirlwind swept through Mitch Helwig's brain. His senses crashed against one another and he fought to regain his balance. But when he spoke, he belied his horror, managing softly, "I'll be right there. Hang on."

Cutting the connection, his hand shaking, he flipped open his address book and punched in another number.

After a couple of beeps, Berenson, the force's mobile equipment manager answered from his home. He looked surprised to see Mitch Helwig, a face from the past, on his screen.

"Karoulis has been shot. I want a copter at his house within ten minutes. Five would be better. Understand?"

"Jesus, Mitch—"

"For Christ's sake, do it! Now!"

"All right."

Mitch gave him the address and directions, and was in his own car within a minute.

*   *   *

At 11:20 P.M., Mitch was at the open door in the front hallway of the Karoulis home. Helen Karoulis was on the floor, her husband cradled in her arms, her face awash in tears.

The ambulance and attendants he had passed at the curb did not seem to be hurrying.

"He's dead," she said. The tears ran in wild rivulets from her eyes.

There was a younger woman on the floor beside her, her face ashen, staring at nothing through a haze of shock.

Mitch saw the tiny burnhole in the shirt over Karoulis's heart.

"He's dead! How can he be dead?" Helen was screaming at him now.

Mitch could hear the Sikorsky's four-bladed main rotor system in the sky nearby, coming closer. The pilot, he knew, would have night-vision goggles, and the copter was equipped with infrared, computer-linked beams, making the city below look like it was high noon.

Looking at Sam Karoulis's face, his head cradled in his wife's arms, his lips parted slightly in death, Mitch heard the man's voice in his head: *I'm your friend.*

The street flooded in light and the copter's blades beat a deafening rhythm as its insectlike body lowered in a wind-blown torrent out of the night sky.

"Dead!" she screamed again.

At the curb, the ambulance attendants were unfolding a trundle.

He closed his eyes and saw a World War One soldier inside a glacier, gliding down through the Italian Alps, year after year, frozen in time. When he opened them he saw the faces of the two women, bathed in anguish, saw his only friend dead.

Blue Limbo.

"Maybe," he said out loud.

The two women stared at him uncomprehendingly.

"Maybe," he breathed again, this time under his breath.

An officer from the copter ran up the walk and stood beside him. "Where to?"

He remembered the conversation with his father. Without turning around, he said "Sunnybrook Hospital." His breathing quickened. "Fast."

"I'm coming too."

Mitch glanced at the younger woman beside Karoulis.

"I'm his daughter. Maria. I'm coming too." She stood up quickly, gaining control of herself.

Mitch was taken aback, but could think of no reason to refuse. "All right." He tilted his head in the direction of the copter.

To Helen Karoulis he said: "Call Huziak. Tell him what happened. Tell him to pick you up and bring you to Sunnybrook."

She stared at him blankly.

"Did you hear me? Are you okay?"

"Yes." She barely breathed the word.

He placed his hand on the small of Maria Karoulis's back, steering her to the waiting copter. "Now. Let's go."

21 On June 12, 1948, Canadian Prime Minister William Lyon Mackenzie King stood on the front steps of the main entrance of Sunnybrook Hospital on Bayview Avenue south of Lawrence, officially opening the largest medical center in the country. CBC Radio carried his words coast to coast: *"Sunnybrook Hospital symbolizes Canada's recognition of the sacrifices made by those members of the armed forces whom this hospital aims to serve, and seeks to honor. . . . My earnest hope is that it may equally express our resolve to share in the building of a better world in which the need for veterans' hospitals will no longer arise."*

Originally intended as parkland in the 1940s, this one-hundred-acre tract fell victim to the needs and priorities of its decade—a decade in which names like Dieppe and Normandy were touchstones.

And thus things changed. The prosthetics unit was internationally known for the design and manufacture of artificial limbs, skull plates, ears, eyes, noses. Bob Hope, Jimmy Durante, Dame Vera Lynn. Queen Elizabeth II, the Queen Mother, princes, princesses. These were typical celebrity visitors from the early years.

And things continued to change. In 1966, in response to a dire need for additional acute care beds and for more hospital teaching programs, the government transferred ownership of Sunnybrook lands and facilities to the University of Toronto for the nominal sum of one silver dollar. Teaching and research blossomed anew. In 1973 it was renamed Sunnybrook Medical Center; in 1988 the Clinical Ethics Center was established, co-ordinating ethics programs for the University's Center for Bioethics. In 1990 it became Sunnybrook Health Science Center, reflecting a new, vast range of services.

And now, in the twenty-first century, the center employed approximately 5,500 full- and part-time staff, the Emergency Department assessed 50,000 patients each year, and there were 400,000 outpatient visits annually to other hospital depart-ments. And on the fifth floor of the Research Building, the Blue Limbo unit had emerged, heralding the twenty-first century with a muted, melancholy note from Azriel's horn.

Mitch Helwig knew none of this. Inside the Sikorsky, peering down onto the center's heliport pad, the rotors pound-ing the still night air with a machine-gun rhythm, he felt his brain fill with molten steel.

He knew that he was somehow dead with Karoulis. But he was not ready to die yet. He would not allow it.

Where's the Blue Limbo unit?"

The eyes of the doctor who was waiting on the heliport landing pad when Mitch Helwig jumped down from the copter widened considerably when he heard the question. "We can't go there. That has to be set up in advance."

"We haven't time for this," Mitch said. "This is a police captain. He's been shot. Take us there, now."

"I wish I could. You don't understand—"

With his left hand, Mitch summoned the attendants wait-ing with the stretcher, while taking out a hand-laser from his pocket with his right hand. He pressed it against the doctor's chest. "Take us there. Now."

"You can't do this. This is crazy—"

"I *am* crazy, Doctor. Don't fuck with me. This is not up for discussion. It's a direct order. Do it or I'm liable to lose my fucking mind right this minute."

The doctor saw the knuckles whiten on the man's hand, saw the distant madness in his eyes, and felt fear. Over the man's shoulder, he saw a young woman climbing down out of the copter.

The attendants were watching silently, immobile at the copter's side.

The doctor nodded to them. They took Karoulis's body from the interior of the Sikorsky, positioning it carefully on the stretcher.

"Follow me," said the doctor.

They placed the body in the waiting ambulance and drove to the Research Building.

When the bedside vidphone beeped at 11:30 P.M., John Krygeri, M.D., Ph.D., was in bed, eyes shut, embracing that transition zone between sleep and waking, reviewing the day's events and dialogues, aligning tomorrow's routines and plans. Surprised, he reached out and answered it quickly.

"Yes?"

"John, it's Stephen Marcus at the center. We've got an emergency here."

Krygeri flipped on the video and stared at the grim face of the young doctor.

"What is it?"

"There's a police officer here with a man alleged to be a police captain. The senior officer has been shot—fatally—by a laser pistol. The officer here insists that we implement the, uh, Blue Limbo mechanism to Revive the man. I explained that everything was closed for the night. He insisted that I contact someone who could get things operational immediately."

"Jesus, what's going on there? We don't operate this way."

Mitch Helwig's face appeared on the screen. He was holding a laser against Stephen Marcus's left cheekbone. "Tell this man what to do until you get here. Then get here quickly."

Krygeri was instantly alert to the anger, madness, and fear that vibrated out of the video images before him. "I'll be right there. Stephen—place the deceased in the cryogenic vault. He'll be fine until I can get there. And officer," he said, addressing Mitch Helwig, "relax. Put that thing away."

Krygeri's wife, sitting up behind him, peered over his shoulder into the screen at the perpetrators of this intrusion.

"Get here," said Mitch, his voice unchanged. "Fast."

John Krygeri, who had held the position of vice president of research at the center for the past three years, had made the Blue Limbo machines his personal crusade. Using clinically trained and Ph.D.-trained researchers paralleling international research development, he had managed to tie into what he thought of as the most dramatic research program in the history of medicine: investigation into life beyond death. He wanted his setup to be superior to all others; he took pride in his personal involvement; the work was exciting and important.

And now this. Perhaps it was inevitable, he thought, looking through the window from the backseat of the cab. People are not rational when a loved one dies.

People are not rational a lot of the rest of the time too, he mused sardonically. Why didn't I call the police? Why? Because they were the police who were involved?

He knew that it was more than that. It was because he had seen the abyss in the man's eyes who had summoned him, the pit of incomprehension and loss. And he had understood. He had been there himself.

The image of his own dead baby floated onto the window through which he was staring, superimposing itself on the reflection of his own face.

He squeezed his eyes shut.

The cab sped on through the night.

* * *

John Krygeri's apparent composure and compassion for the events of the evening caught Mitch Helwig slightly off guard. He had expected complete opposition, the sludge of bureaucracy, anticipated the worst. Instead, he was confronted by a man who seemed to be genuinely interested, who wanted to help. And because he sensed that the interest was real, he began to relax.

Mitch Helwig explained what had happened in short terse phrases. The young woman, who was the dead man's daughter, added an occasional contribution.

Krygeri turned to the young doctor, who, standing nervously to one side, had listened with growing fascination. "Stephen," he asked, "would you like to help?"

The young doctor looked surprised.

"Yes or no?" asked Krygeri.

"I don't know what to do."

"I'll show you."

The young man nodded, dazzled by the rush of events. "All right." He stepped forward. "I'll help."

"Good." Krygeri turned to Mitch and Maria. "Let's get started. This will take most of the night."

It took more than most of the night.

Mitch Helwig and Maria Karoulis, propped by caffeine and adrenaline, watched most of the proceedings between the pendulum swing of shock and clinical detachment. Shortly after their own arrival, Helen Karoulis, still in shock, arrived with Huziak. When the surgery began she was unable to cope, and Huziak took her to an adjoining waiting room, where they spent the next few hours. At three A.M., Huziak rose to leave.

"Call me, Mitch. Keep me posted."

Mitch nodded. He squeezed the man's hand warmly. "Thanks."

Huziak, looking suddenly old, squeezed back. He hesitated, then turned and left.

Mitch and Maria understood little of what passed before their eyes. There was the initial cutting, the drilling, the ultrasonic aspirator, the insertion of electrodes into various points of the brain, the artificial cerebrospinal fluid—replacing lost fluid— pumped into cranial cavities. The brain itself was moist, cobwebbed with filaments, all an ultraviolet purple under the operating lights. Marcus took a bulb and squirted some water over it, while Krygeri donned a pair of glasses with small microscopes attached to the lenses and zeroed in for the fine work.

To see the human body suddenly demystified into a machine capable of adjustment and maintenance and repair left Mitch with a tangle of emotions and insights. He had never witnessed surgery before, never seen an autopsy. Although his stomach proved equal to the experience, his mind reeled with questions.

There was more mystery here than ever before.

Staring into the opalescent purple neural matter, beneath the membranous layers, underneath the skull, Mitch felt himself descending into the mystery. Is Karoulis's life in here? How can a surge of electricity light up a memory, a thought, a feeling? What are we tampering with?

He had no answers.

At six A.M., two additional surgeons appeared, having been summoned by Krygeri an hour before. Thus pushed back from the center of activity, and informed that there would be many more hours of precision work, Mitch and Maria joined Helen in the waiting room. Silently, sitting beside her, Maria put her stepmother's head on her shoulder and stroked her hair. It was a union that excluded him, and in his isolation, Mitch finally felt the exhaustion that went deep into his bones.

Karoulis's daughter met his eyes, the life drained from her face.

"Let's go," he said.

"Where?"

"Coffee. Some food maybe. We'll come back."

She hesitated. "I can't eat."

Helen merely shook her head.

"You have to. We have to." He paused. "We'll come back," he repeated.

Helen waved him off. "Thank you, Mitch. I'm staying."

He looked again at Maria.

She nodded, dropped her eyes. "All right."

"We'll bring you something," he said to Helen.

She smiled weakly, indifferent, but grateful for the thought. "Go," she said. "I'll be here." Her eyes were hollow. "We'll be waiting," she said, "Sam and I."

Mitch knew that Fran's Restaurant at Yonge and Eglinton never closed, so they went there. Over a light breakfast, he looked more carefully at this woman who was Karoulis's daughter and was more impressed by her calm, controlled nature and good sense than he was by what was obviously an attractive woman beneath the haggard exterior.

"Why are you doing this?" she asked.

"Breakfast? Because we need food."

"No. All of it. The Revival. Everything."

Mitch's eyes, heavy-lidded with exhaustion, brightened with an inner flare. "Because he was my friend," he said. Then he changed it. "Because he is my friend."

"Why was he shot? Why did someone want to kill him?"

The flare behind the eyes surged. "Because he is my friend," he said. "Because he helped me. That's why."

Maria Karoulis stared with growing fascination at the

man opposite her. She saw the fatigue leave him, replaced by an anvil of resolve and strength.

"I won't let them. I won't leave them alone," he said.

She continued to stare at him.

"It's not over. Not at all."

Did you understand what you were seeing back there?" he asked.

"I watched. I saw it. I don't know if anyone can understand it, even the doctors."

Mitch ran a finger around the edge of his coffee cup. "You know it's only temporary."

She nodded. "I know." Then she said, "He's my father. I'm going to lose my father."

Mitch dropped his eyes.

She put a hand to her forehead, peered at him through her own red, swollen eyes. "I can't believe the feelings, what I'm feeling."

Mitch said nothing.

"I'm shaking."

He reached across and took her hand, motivated by simple compassion. And because she sensed the sincerity of his gesture, she accepted it.

I had a friend," she said, "a doctor, who worked at the Montreal Neurological Institute and Hospital. Mostly he worked on people with common epilepsy, who had seizures caused by electrical disturbances in the brain. His job was to get into the limbic system of the brain and excise the flawed area. During an operation he would sometimes stimulate the patient's brain with an electrical probe. Because the brain has no sense of touch, sometimes only a local anesthetic was used. These people would actually be awake during surgery. He told me that at the probe's touch, many patients would often report bizarre hallucinations, feelings of déjà vu, spontaneous flashbacks. An old woman told him she was listening to an orchestra playing *La Bohème*. She could hum it, and stopped only when he removed the probe."

She stopped abruptly, thinking her own thoughts, giving him time to digest.

"So you ask me if I understood what I was seeing back there." She paused. "I don't think anyone understands what they're seeing in cases like that."

Mitch nodded. In his head he heard his own father's voice, wily and perceptive, confirming her thoughts: *The brain . . . who can figure it?*

22

Mitch was sitting in the waiting room with Helen and Maria when John Krygeri finally came in to join them. It was 10:30 A.M. The doctor seated himself heavily in a chair across from them, sighing deeply.

They waited.

"We believe everything went well," he said. "There were no complications."

They were silent for a moment. Then it was Maria who spoke. "What does that mean? What happens next?"

"We'll wait until the nutrients and acid-balancing agents introduced into the blood stabilize, then we can activate communication. The chip—the electrode—implanted outside the dura will send brain signals from the cochlea to the computer terminal. The terminal we have will then analyze, synthesize, and translate—transform the signals into spoken English, which we will be able to hear quite clearly. By speaking directly into the computer's microphone attachment, we can then reverse the process. In this way, we can converse, as it were, with the subject."

"When will this be possible?" asked Mitch.

"Later this evening. Perhaps tomorrow morning."

"But he's still dead. He's not coming back." Maria's voice sifted her own statements, her face a puzzled frown.

"We can maintain this state for about four weeks

maximum. After that amount of time it has always faded away. We're still searching for answers."

"He's dead, then," she repeated.

John Krygeri stared at the three of them, seeming to weigh his thoughts, his words. "I don't know," he said. "I truly don't know. This is terra incognita, Ms. Karoulis. We've got to think about a lot of things in a new way." He ran both his hands through his hair, down to the nape, and began rubbing his own neck. "Some two-thousand-year-old seeds were taken from an ancient tomb in central China back in the mid-1980s. They stunned archaeologists and biologists by sprouting into plants bearing tomatoes." He continued to rub his neck. "University of Alberta scientists managed to revive bacteria from members of the historic Franklin expedition who perished mysteriously back in 1845." He folded his hands in his lap and seemed to decide, in an instant of spontaneous empathy, to tell them his own story. His eyes softened. "My wife and I had a baby, five years ago. He was born prematurely, weighed only two pounds—a kilo. He was pronounced dead moments after he was born. No noticeable heartbeat, no brain activity, nothing. Later in the day, when the funeral home worker arrived to pick up the body, he began crying. Just like that. Crying."

No one said anything.

"The hair stood up on the back of my neck. No one could believe it—or explain it." He was quiet a moment. "He lived another twenty-four hours."

They continued to listen in silence.

Mitch watched the doctor's brow furrow as details and memories, kept buried, resurfaced, animating his eyes.

"That was a turning point for me." Krygeri stared at the wall while he stretched his legs out in front of him, sighing with exhaustion and emotion. "So," he said, "you ask me if your father is dead, and I tell you that I do not know. There is so much that we do not know. My answer is meant to be neither placatory nor fatuous. The mystery is there. It is indeed there."

"He's alive," Helen Karoulis said.

Maria and Mitch turned to look at her.

Serenity settled into her face.

"My Sam," she repeated, "is alive."

At 11:00 A.M., Mitch was on the vidphone.

Huziak's face blossomed on the screen. "Mitch," he said, "what's happening?"

"It's done."

Huziak did not respond.

"But it'll be later tonight or tomorrow before we can attempt communication."

Unable to mask amazement, the staff sergeant's lips parted.

"What's happening there?" Mitch asked.

Huziak shook off the stupor. "I've kept my mouth shut, but everyone knows somethin's up. Where's Karoulis? I keep gettin' asked. We're even gettin' some calls from the press. Some of them have got wind of it. Maybe from neighbors, maybe from hospital sources, who knows?"

"You got three or four men you can trust?"

"Yeah. I guess so."

"Assign them here, to me. We'll need him guarded around the clock."

"I don't know if I can do that, Mitch."

"Do it. Or Karoulis is probably dead—for good—taking anything he knows with him."

"Jesus, Mitch—"

"Or I'm probably dead too."

Huziak's jaw tightened and he was breathing heavily.

"Remember the explosion in his office?"

Huziak nodded grudgingly.

"That wasn't supposed to involve you. It was meant for him and me. You know that."

Huziak nodded again. Then he inhaled and exhaled deeply to regain composure. "I'll send four uniformed officers. I'll take responsibility."

"Huziak."

"Yeah?"

"I owe you. Again." He smiled.

"Everybody owes everybody. Big fucking deal," he said. Again.

At 11:30 A.M., four uniformed officers emerged from the elevator. Maria, Helen, and the hospital staff watched silently as Mitch deployed the men in different strategic positions. Two were taken downstairs to the main floor entrances, the remaining two left on the fifth floor. Mitch introduced them to John Krygeri, explaining that no one was to enter the area where Karoulis was being kept without Krygeri's or his own approval.

Turning to the two women, he said, "You could leave now. Go home. Get some sleep."

"I'm staying," Helen said.

"It'll be later tonight or tomorrow morning, Helen, before anything happens. You should get some rest."

"You must be kidding, Mitch. Rest?" She smiled weakly.

Mitch returned the meek smile, nodded, understanding. Then, to Maria: "What about you?"

"What are you going to do?"

"Get something to eat. Run a few errands. Some loose ends." His face was noncommital.

"I'm coming with you."

"I could take you home."

"I'd like to come with you. I'd like to know more. I think you can tell me more." Her voice remained even and persistent.

He considered. "All right," he said. "Let's go."

Mitch gave the cabdriver the address on Glen Manor.

"Why are we going to my father's house?" Maria asked, beside him.

"My car is still there."

"Is that important now?"

"There are things in my car. Things I may need." He did not elaborate.

When he opened the trunk of his Chev, Maria peered in with discreet curiosity. There were several full green garbage bags visible.

Mitch lifted one out and closed the trunk. "Let's go inside."

Once inside the door, Mitch headed into the living room. The television was still on where Sam Karoulis had been sitting the night before.

The night before? Mitch thought. Had it only been the night before? It felt as if years had passed, as if his life had telescoped to an unimaginable point far beyond anything that he could have foreseen a mere twenty-four hours ago.

Mitch clicked the set off.

When he began to unbutton his shirt, Maria's eyes widened.

He saw her reaction. "Excuse me," he said. Turning his back, he continued to take off his shirt, draping it across the back of the sofa. Then he reached into the green plastic bag and pulled out a heavy T-shirt of some sort. He shrugged into it, pulled it down to his waist, and began to put his shirt back on over top of the new undergarment.

Maria watched. "Bulletproof," she said.

He was buttoning up the shirt. "Trade name is the Silent Guard. About two kilos. Ten layers of thirty-one by thirty-one count, one thousand denier, with a solid, foil-thin, alloy interior layer." He looked at her. "Laserproof. Or, as close to laserproof as we've got. It would take a bit of time for a laser to burn through—maybe enough time for a person to take cover, or rush the assailant."

He watched her face draw sober.

"Your father was killed by a laser. I think they'll try to kill me too." He finished tucking his shirt into his pants. The shirt was loose-fitting enough so that the Guard did not show. "I'm sure that you're safe," he said. "Can't see any reason why you wouldn't be."

"This is madness."

Mitch took time to look at her, because he had no good answer. He saw a young woman who had tumbled into her worst nightmare, a surreal series of mishaps; her world had turned upside down, and she was struggling not to spin off this new planet's suddenly reversed gravity.

He looked around the home that was no longer a home, thought how it would never be the same for Maria or her mother. Like him, they had been involved somehow in a cataclysmic explosion that had destroyed the past, permanently and irretrievably.

She was shaking her head.

23 "What's going on? Why is this happening?" Mitch Helwig stared across the table at Maria Karoulis and let seconds tick by before attempting to answer her question. They were in a diner on the north side of Queen near Pape that served an all-day breakfast. He was grateful for the appearance of the waitress with their orders of bacon, eggs, orange juice and coffee, because it postponed trying to explain all this. When the waitress moved off, however, Maria was still staring at him, still waiting.

"My best guess?"

She waited.

"Your father and I worked together last fall to destroy a central underworld warehouse in the city. Among others, a key underworld figure was killed." He paused, then added: "I killed him." He drank some coffee, began eating the food in front of him.

Maria lifted her coffee to her lips, listening, her jaw clenched tightly.

"I couldn't have succeeded without your father's direct help and involvement. It just happened that way."

"But surely my father's been responsible, directly or indirectly, for the demise of hundreds, thousands of criminal ventures over the course of his career. What made this one different?"

"It was bigger. Much bigger. Probably international in

scope. It must have cost this particular consortium literally billions of dollars." His eyes clouded as he remembered.

"Billions!"

"Yes."

"What kind of business could operate in the billions—out of a warehouse?"

He spread some jam on the toast. "You'd be surprised. A ton of coke on the street's worth about five billion. There were at least five tons in this particular warehouse that we knew of. There was probably lots more."

Maria's eyes widened as she grasped the numbers.

The food felt good, slowly filling his stomach. "There were automobiles, guns—the old-fashioned kind—and lasers—six thousand of them—stolen from a local armory in a military-type raid in which seven men were killed. And these guys had portfolios arranged by lawyers: IBM stock, Bell Telephone, breweries, Xerox . . . You know, legitimate, blue-chip stuff. All to cover the filth, the stench of the business. Some prostitution, gambling, kiddie porn, snuff features—"

"What?"

"—and even a black market in human organs."

"I don't even understand what I'm hearing."

"That's because you're a decent, normal human being. You haven't lived with the same trash that your father and I have."

"My father was killed by the people behind all this?"

"I think so."

"Who are they?"

He wiped his mouth with a napkin. "Don't know exactly. You never seem to get at the brain of an organism like this, just the tentacles." He thought about it. "Your father and I tried to make a difference. We think we did."

"And now he's paying for it."

"I think so."

"You think so!"

He watched the anger flash in her eyes, understanding it in a clean way; it was people like the ones he had just described to her that he could never understand.

"I think everybody pays for everything, somehow. We did what was right. We did what we had to do." He watched her face, pale and drawn. "Your father is a fine man."

Shaking, she took a long sip of the hot coffee.

"As long as there have been cops, there have been cops on the take. It's the nature of the viral infections that infest any organism. But there are some, high up in the force, who live very well. Who ignored the business I've described to you. They're more than viruses. They're a cancer. I think they're at the root of this." He remembered the explosion that had almost claimed Karoulis and Huziak. Who else but a cop could have gotten into Karoulis's office?

"Back in the nineties, an underworld gang ten times the size of the American mafia began making inroads into Canada: the Yakuza, Japanese based. Boasted more than a hundred thousand members, bought up legitimate businesses in the U.S., and formed alliances with the American mafia and Korean and Chinese drug gangs. Could be them. Could be somebody else. They're all out there, somewhere."

Maria had her coffee cup cradled in both hands on the table in front of her, as if for warmth.

It was when Mitch made a left, turning south onto Carlaw from Queen, that he noticed it.

The black car.

Maybe, he thought, I'm imagining it. Maybe I've had too little sleep or too much caffeine or am just strung out too tight.

Or maybe it's really there.

Instead of turning right at Eastern Avenue and heading west to the Bayview extension and back to Sunnybrook, he went through the lights and continued south. When he failed to turn right at Lake Shore Boulevard, continuing farther down into the industrial area at the city's southeastern protrusion into the Outer Harbor, Maria glanced at him sharply.

"What's wrong?"

He could see it in the rearview mirror, still coming on behind him, unwavering.

"Not sure," he said. "Give me a few more minutes."

He saw her watching his face, his eyes flicking from hers, then back and forth quickly between the mirror and the front windshield.

The day was gray, promising rain. Directly ahead of them rose the Hearn Generator Tower, the bleak city landmark, a cement smokestack that rose upward grimly, barren sentinel of the uninhabitable urbanscape that they were entering. Even in the daytime, the two halogen white lights near its peak continued to flash rhythmically, alerting aircraft to its presence.

Mitch made a right onto Commissioners Street.

Thirty seconds or so later, the black car rounded the corner as well.

Ahead of them lay a wide strip of little-traveled pavement, unbroken by a stop sign or traffic light, almost a kilometer in length. Steel, four-armed hydroelectric towers straddled a middle boulevard, feeding the fenced in, low colorless structures on both sides: oil refineries, recycling mills, a rendering plant.

Mitch drove steadily ahead, stopped when the road ended at Cherry Street, turned left. When he crossed the lift-bridge over the channel, glanced down at the brown water and barges, he sensed the unreality of his footing. This was all landfill, artificial solidity, a place that nature had not intended to exist, spreading like an oil spill from the city out into Lake Ontario.

In his rearview mirror, he saw the black car loom up over the bridge behind him.

He made a left at Unwin Avenue, his last chance to turn before the road ended at Clark Beach Park—what had been called Cherry Beach when he was growing up. He remembered going there as a kid with his parents and swimming. Taking Barbie there one day a few summers ago had hammered home the passage of time: the park had been acceptable, but the beach, like all the city beaches along the lake, had lost its magic. Pollution signs were posted everywhere.

The Metro Police Department K-9 Corps building was on the southeast corner, where it had been reestablished after an absence of years.

"Pull in there," Maria said.

Mitch continued east. The building was fading behind them.

"What's the matter with you?" The fear crackled in her voice now. "He won't follow us in there!"

"I know."

"What are you doing? This is crazy!"

The giant Hearn cement phallus dominated the sky ahead of them, its lights flashing like the beat of blood driven from the heart. On the right was a set of rusted, unused railroad tracks, then acres of scrub brush that had managed to take root in the fill of sand, cinders, cement, and chemicals that petered down to the lake. On their left they passed a factory and wire-fenced yard with a painted sign that read BRISTOL METAL INDUSTRIES, "THE RECYCLING PEOPLE."

"We'd have lost him if we'd turned in there," he said. "He would have kept going, disappeared."

"I'd have thought that was the idea!" She had turned to watch out the rear window openly now. The black car rounded the corner behind them, still coming.

"He'd have come back again. Tonight. Tomorrow. Next week. I might not have spotted him the next time. This is our best chance." He turned to stare at her astonished face. "You see," he said, "right now he thinks he's the hunter."

Maria stared at him, speechless.

Above them, flocks of seagulls circled randomly, squawking and screeching, riding the updrafts from the wind that had sprung up off the darkening lake.

The road curved around the fence that bore the sign, RICHARD L. HEARN THERMAL GENERATING STATION. They were at the base of the monstrous gray urban volcano. All about them was debris that might have been spewed from the ashes and smoke of its white-tipped peak.

A single-lane bridge traversing a canal squeezed the pavement ahead: MAXIMUM WEIGHT, 25 TONNES. Coming off the bridge, Mitch spotted the sign and road that he had been awaiting: OUTER HARBOR MARINA.

He turned right. A quick glance in the rearview mirror confirmed that his new course had been noted.

Fucker, he thought. *Just keep coming.* He felt the molten steel that had filled his brain when he realized what had happened to Karoulis begin to boil anew. *Hunt me, you fucker. Come on.*

Maria sat motionless beside him.

The land beneath him, dumped into the lake by thousands of trucks, flattened for years by the groan of bulldozers, stretched ahead of him in curves and landscaped hillocks. On his left, a raft of neckless starlings covered the hydro wires, stilled against the rain promised by the misted, slate sky; on the right, the black, choppy water of the harbor stretched back to Cherry Beach. A single sail headed for shore. Above it all, the CN Tower watched, its spire hidden in the haze.

Mitch drove for about a kilometer, passing parking lots and hosts of masts at dock. Then the pavement suddenly ended, turning to gravel. Piles of cement blocks lined the sides of the road ahead, and directly ahead to his left a huge pyramid of sand rose up to a peak some ten meters high. A new

sign was propped at the gravel road's edge: DANGER, CON-
STRUCTION SITE, KEEP OUT.

He slowed, but did not stop. Easing onto the gravel, he
inched ahead to the edge of the sand pyramid, then pulled the
car off through the scrub and debris until it was nestled behind the earthen mound, hidden from the road.

He stopped and waited.

Maria said nothing.

Within a few minutes, the black car—a Buick, Mitch
noted—passed slowly by. There was a single male driver
within. Mitch waited until it disappeared out of sight down the
gravel road.

"Come on," he said, opening the door. "You can help."

"Help do what?" She followed him to the road.

He began lifting and carrying the cement construction
blocks from the piles by the roadside and placing them directly
in the road, obstructing the path. Maria quickly imitated him.

"That's a dead end," he said, nodding in the direction
that the black vehicle had gone. "It ends at the lake. Half a kilometer or so."

She picked another block up and placed it on the road.
"So we're locking him in. He has to come back this way."

"That's right." He continued to lift and carry. With the
weight and heft in his hands, he recalled the blocks he had
hauled up the stairs to make Barbie's desk, and the sudden
thought of his daughter made his hands clench, steeling him
further.

He knew he was doing what had to be done. There was
no choice. Like the dead end down which he had lured his pur-
suer, his own options had somehow constricted to this: the
coin-flip of life and death, on a mutated, ashen peninsula that
coiled slowly out onto this dead lake.

The lights from the giant smokestack flashed rhythmically behind him.

He stood back, wiped his hands, studied the mien of the
young woman beside him. Her coolness and rapid appraisal of

the situation made things easier on both of them. He was grateful for her composure, aware of the value of such intelligence and control.

She looked at him, eyes piercing, the wind from the lake, cold now, catching a strand of hair, blowing it across her face.

"Back to the Chev," he said. "Both of us."

She nodded and turned.

His own eyes narrowed and locked in the direction from which the black car would reappear.

Take this." He handed her the rifle from the trunk, extracting the folding shoulder-stock.

"Good Lord." She rolled it over in her hands.

"It's a Sanyo laser. Maximum heat, maximum distance. Just squeeze the trigger. You don't have to hit your target like you do with a bullet. The blue beam will tell you where you're aiming, and if you just hold down the trigger, you can cut your target down by sweeping across it."

"This isn't standard police issue."

"Does that matter now?" He lifted the nylon shoulder harness with the two water tanks and pistol attachment out of the green plastic bag, began shrugging into it.

"What's that?"

He pressed the Velcro tabs on his chest, checked the dial on the pistol's side. "Water gun," he said.

"What—"

"Shh. We got company."

Over a small rise in the road, the black Buick loomed up against the lead slab that was the sky.

The car stopped at the barrier of cement blocks. Inside, the man appeared to remain motionless.

Mitch set the dial on his pistol for thirty milliamps. The

man in the car interested him; he would be worth questioning.
I hope, he thought, that neither Maria with the laser nor a
higher amperage on this baby will be necessary. "Stay here. Be
careful."

She clutched the black plastic rifle tightly.

"Watch everything."

She nodded, her mouth grim.

He stepped out into the open.

Inside the car, the man's head turned to face him.

Finally, Mitch thought. One of the jackals, face-to-face.
A visible opponent.

Both the front and rear power windows on the passenger
side facing Mitch slid down while the man continued to stare
at him. Mitch, his pistol at ready, strode forward in slow, measured paces.

Because his eyes were fixed on the stranger's face, the bolt
of blue that tracked onto his chest from the rear seat took
Mitch Helwig totally by surprise. In the next single second, he
winced at the surge of heat that would have killed him instantly
if he had not been wearing the Silent Guard, smelled the acrid
smoke coming from the searing puncture on his chest as the
beam tried to eat its way through the unexpected barrier, and
spotted the gas-dynamic CO_2 laser, bolted in the storage space
beneath the car's rear window, which was fixed on him. Dashboard controls, he thought, realizing that the man's hands were
out of sight.

In the next second, he saw the confusion in his opponent's
eyes because his victim was still alive, heard Maria shout his
name, and flung himself to the ground, rolling sideways. When
he stopped, the Buick's laser had shut off, and a cobalt beam
from Maria's Sanyo spanned the dead space between the two
vehicles. It tracked onto the front fender, cracking the metal
with the tearing sound of a giant can opener, as Mitch heard
the Buick's engine fire up.

"The tires!" he shouted. "Hit the tires!"

The crystal blue beam shifted to the front tire, which exploded within a second, then to the rear tire, which detonated with equal force.

Through the smoke, Mitch saw the man's face staring out at him as the vehicle listed onto its two side rims like a ship that had run a reef. The laser beam above him blinked out as suddenly as it had appeared. Mitch watched as the man inside the car frantically began to work controls on the dashboard.

Without waiting to find out what else might happen, Mitch, still on his stomach, aimed his water pistol and squeezed the trigger.

He sprayed the vehicle from side to side, aware of how ineffectual it all looked. But some of it got through the open windows and struck the driver. He saw the man's back go rigid, saw the cords in his neck stand out as his mouth opened and his eyes rolled back in his skull, the electrical current bolting him into unconsciousness.

Mitch dragged the man from the driver's seat by the back of his belt and jacket collar, across the gravel and cinders, and propped him up against the sand pile where Maria was standing, waiting. She seemed calm enough, the rifle still tucked professionally into the nook between arm and shoulder.

"You ever use one of those before?" he asked.

"No."

"Ever use a gun of any kind?"

She shook her head.

Mitch looked into her eyes, which were coolly distant. For a moment, he felt the chill wind of her gaze, saw the angry storm. "You did good."

"Did he kill my father?" She stared down at the buckled figure.

Mitch was headed for the Chev. "Don't know yet."

"Is he dead?" Her voice was neutral.

"No. I sent an electric shock through his system that

knocked him senseless. He may never be quite the same. But he's not dead." He paused. "Not yet." Then he stopped and looked at her. "You want to kill him?"

She nodded. "Yes."

He touched the smoldering burn where the laser had struck him, felt the thin alloy between living and dying, and took his fingers away when they began to burn, like the simmering anger that filled his chest. He nodded in agreement. "I know," he said.

She looked at him.

He opened the Chev's door, reaching for the duffel bag on the floor of the backseat. "I know."

24

Maria Karoulis watched as Mitch Helwig lifted the calculator-sized device from the duffel bag and hooked it on the front of his belt. She saw him run the wire from it inside his shirt and press the sticky electrode onto the bare skin of his side.

"Is that what I think it is?" she asked.

"What do you think it is?"

"One of those lie-detector things. A Barking Dog."

"It is." He focused the Dog's eye, adjusting the range.

She shook her head. "Lasers, Barking Dogs, electric water guns, laser shields. Is this legal? I don't get it. You're not supposed to have any of this stuff."

"If I didn't have it, we'd be dead now."

She had no answer.

"Look at what they've got." He nodded toward the Buick. "Car's equipped with a small laser cannon, rear-mounted, controlled from the dashboard. If we take the time to check the vehicle out, we'll find lots more, I guarantee. Your father was killed with a laser. This is an organization that has a working capital in the *billions* of dollars, remember? They use technology to eliminate people like us. And we run after them with Smith and Wesson thirty-eights." He paused, controlling himself. "They *count* on us operating within the predictable legal system that they've learned to manipulate and with the antiquated weaponry at our disposal." Realizing that he might be rambling too much, he sighed. "I'm a wild card in the deck. The only rules I know are the ones that make sense, the ones that simplify." He straightened. The Dog was ready. "The ones that lead to the truth." He saw the flicker of doubt in her eyes. "I don't look for anyone's approval," he added.

She was watching him, her eyes riveted.

"Sunnybrook—where we took your father."

"What about it?"

"He's in the right place. It used to be a veteran's hospital. He's a veteran, a casualty of a new kind of war."

The man at their feet was stirring, twitching his arms and legs.

Mitch looked down at him. "We all are."

The man on the ground struggled onto his elbows, shaking the fuzziness from his brain. Mitch placed him in his early thirties, tall, strong, experienced at intimidation, accustomed to the financial perks of his work, judging from his tailored suit and well-manicured nails. Jamming the water pistol in his belt, Mitch held out his hand in Maria's direction for the laser rifle. She passed it to him.

The man groaned, rolled onto his side, struggled to rise, blinked several times in an exaggerated manner. Finally, he focused on Mitch and Maria and actually managed to sit up, the pain and residual soreness from his shock evident in the smallest movement. He sighed, hunching forward, his arms resting on his knees.

Mitch stood so that the Barking Dog took it all in. Only questions that it could assess were necessary.

He asked the question that mattered. "Did you kill Sam Karoulis?"

The man looked at him, saw the Barking Dog, understood. He remained silent.

Mitch raised the Sanyo, sighting it on him. "I'll ask it again. If you don't answer, I'll kill you."

"You're a cop." The voice held disdain. "You won't kill me. You don't operate that way."

Mitch shook his head. "Thinking like that would be a big mistake."

Maria turned to look at Mitch.

The stranger seemed to note her uncertainty. Clearly accustomed to doing the intimidating, he now stared back with insolence at his captors, gaining confidence with their civilized hesitation.

"What you don't understand is that I'm crazy," Mitch Helwig said. He shrugged the Sanyo into the crook of his shoulder and turned it on a two-meter-long piece of discarded lumber propped a few arms' lengths from the stranger against the sandpile. The steel-blue heat beam flared to life soundlessly as he squeezed the trigger, and with a steady, sure hand, he burned the word *crazy* into the wood. When it was complete, he let the trigger go and the beam disappeared, leaving only the smoking and crackling of the wood to disturb the stillness of the tableau.

He turned to the man.

The stranger's eyes signaled a new uncertainty. His face became grimmer.

Mitch trained the rifle deliberately and calmly on the man. "You've been watching too much television," he said. "Your putrid, fucked-up excuse for a brain has absorbed one-hour cop shows like a dull sponge for so long that you figure this is just another part to be played out. You figure you know how it'll come out because you've seen it so often that you can't even think beyond the commercials. You'd kill me, but I'm not supposed to kill you." He shook his head. "You poor stupid fuck."

Bending his knees, Mitch reached into the duffel bag at his feet and withdrew the bionic, silver hand and severed triceps that he had cut from the Chinese youth who had also tried to kill him.

Straightening, he tossed it on the ground, halfway between himself and his captive, where it lay, grotesquely, palm upward, its silver finish hypnotic.

All eyes fixed on it.

The man licked his lips. "What's that?"

"Last guy I dealt with was luckier than you. He'd already lost his hand. But," he said, "it still hurt when this came off." Mitch paused, as if thinking. "Maybe you can have it after I take off your hand. Save you some money." He began to sight the rifle, with exaggerated care, on the man's forearm. "I'll try to get as close to the same spot as I can." He closed one eye.

Maria's lips parted, then closed again.

"Wait." The word burst from the man like a gunshot.

Mitch opened the eye. With the gun still sighted, he waited.

There was both anger and fear in the man's eyes now. He worked his jaw, breathing deeply.

Mitch waited.

"What do you want to know?" He was breathing in fits, his efforts to calm himself failing.

Mitch lowered the Sanyo halfway, just enough to acknowledge the concession. He repeated the question: "Did you kill Sam Karoulis?"

Maria held her breath, her entire body tensed, as she waited for the answer.

"No."

The Barking Dog sent Mitch Helwig only the mildest tremor of cold, a tickle.

"But you know who did."

"Not exactly."

Nothing. The truth.

"What does that mean?"

"It means simply that I don't know exactly who did it. Orders move vertically downward. There's little horizontal communication. It could have been any one of many. I'm not your guy." The frustration in his tone was overt.

The Barking Dog let it pass.

Maria surprised both of them by asking the next question. "Who gives your orders?" Her own anger was out in the open now.

The man remained silent.

Without thinking, Maria took two steps closer to the man before firing the same question, this time a little louder: "Who gives your orders?"

It was the break that the man had been waiting for. Hunched forward, arms on knees, he was able to uncoil like a catapult toward Maria before Mitch could bring the rifle up to sight it. His left hand clamped on her calf, and her mouth opened and her eyes widened in sudden shock and pain as she fell to her right knee. The man quickly pulled himself behind her, and when he removed his left hand from her calf and placed it in a closed fist at her neck, Mitch saw the blood pour forth from her leg. A quick glance back at the man's left fist revealed the silver ring with the two-centimeter-long, needle-sharp straight-claw pressed against Maria's jugular vein. He had seen such rings previously only in training exercises: high-density steel alloy, one piece, shaped like the symbol for "male," but with the barb removed from the prong. It was worn on the little finger, with the point directed inward against the palm, covered with a quickly removable rubber sheath.

Mitch cursed himself for having missed it. And he cursed himself again for letting Maria fall into the man's clutches. *I'm* the experienced one, he thought. This is all on my shoulders.

A tiny trickle of blood slid from the ring's point where it pressed against the soft flesh of Maria's neck.

The man's eyes were hard, desperate. "I'll kill her." His teeth were bared now, his breath ragged.

There was no more waiting.

In the space of a second, Mitch sighted on the man's forehead and pressed the trigger. The blue pencil-beam flashed into life, its heat-death instantaneous. Even as the seconds tripped by, as the man's grip on Maria relaxed and she lunged forward, out of his grasp, Mitch did not release the trigger. If anything, he squeezed it more tightly, with greater fury.

The hole in the man's skull widened and boiled as the lifeless body slumped forward onto its face.

"Mitch!"

Her shout brought him back. Blinking, he released the trigger. His heart was pounding and the air felt cold.

He turned to look at her. There were no tears, no hysteria—perhaps because the inevitability of what had happened was obvious in retrospect. But there was anguish and confusion in her face. The dark path down which she had been pushed was ruthless and unyielding, the stakes fundamentally primal. And, unlike him, she had never trod this path before.

He watched the wind from across the black water make her hunch and shiver.

Where are we going?" The Chev was headed back into the city.

Mitch was thinking. "My place." Then he added, "For now." He remembered the black car, how it had trailed him from dropping Barbie off at his former apartment in Thorncliffe to his father's residence on Yonge Street. They know, he thought, where my daughter and father live. And this bothered him much more than the fact that they could easily find him at his own place.

The black car itself, even though their quick search just now had been cursory, had yielded no new information.

"We won't be able to speak with your father until tonight. We've got hours to kill. We have to go someplace. It's only five minutes from here."

"Give me a weapon," she said.

He glanced sideways at her.

She returned his glance, a new hardness carved in her features.

He reached into his pocket. "Keep this." He handed her the Bausch & Lomb hand-laser.

She took it without saying anything, studied it briefly, pocketed it. Then, twisting her left leg up onto the seat beside her, she examined the puncture in her calf. It was still bleeding slightly, and because it had streaked the length of her leg to her shoe, looked much worse than it was. She took a tissue from her purse, wet it with her tongue, and cleaned up as much of the area as she could. Again, rummaging about in her purse, she came up with a Band-Aid and taped it across another tissue, covering the wound.

In spite of himself, Mitch saw not only the injury being treated, but the feminine leg twisting from beneath the skirt. When he caught himself staring at it more than was necessary, he forced his concentration back to the road. How, he wondered, can I be so easily distracted, with what's going on all around me? How much effect is this woman having on me?

He realized again that his father was right. Apparently, there was no understanding the brain.

When they pulled up in front of Mitch's apartment, he reached into the backseat for the duffel bag.

Maria watched him. "What else have you got in there?"

He lifted it onto his lap before opening the door. I hope, he thought, the difference between success and failure. Between living and dying. Aloud, he said: "Tools of the trade."

Standing on the landing outside the third-floor apartment, Mitch put his finger to his lips and shook his head.

Maria nodded.

He pulled the bug detector from the bag and quietly opened the door. They stepped inside.

Moving it from side to side, Mitch watched the dial begin to sniff out low, high, and UHF frequencies. It swung upward dramatically as he walked to the phone. Bending, he snapped the cord from its wall jack, and the dial in his hand settled back into its comfort zone.

N

He walked through the galley kitchen into the living area before the dial began to rise upward once more. It peaked when he moved into the southwest corner; kneeling down, he placed the unit on the floor and lifted the corner of the room's poorly placed broadloom. Beneath it was the bug, battery operated, the size of a watch face, which he recognized as capable of transmitting to an FM receiver several kilometers away. He picked it up, went to the skylight, pushed it open, and hurled the device as far as he could into a neighbor's backyard.

With Maria behind him, he entered the bathroom, then the two bedrooms.

Nothing.

He paced off the entire apartment once more. Still nothing.

He clicked it off. "It's okay now."

Returning to the front door, he placed the monitor back into his bag, lifting it and bringing it inside with him.

When he closed the door behind him, Maria heard it click, and relaxed, ever so slightly.

A haven, however temporary, was welcome.

25 It wasn't until she was alone with him, in the place where he lived, that Maria Karoulis realized how little she knew about this man. Everything had happened so quickly. The most dramatic moments of her life, the most intense series of emotions, she had played out with a virtual stranger—a man totally unlike anyone she had ever met— even the antithesis of anyone she had ever wanted to meet.

Yet she was comfortable with him. She trusted him. So, obviously, did Helen, and so had her father.

Looking at him staring through the skylight, she recalled his words: *I don't look for anyone's approval.* She thought about herself, about her desire to go to Madagascar, about her graduate work at McGill, and wondered if there might be more in the way of common overlap in their personalities than was at first evident.

He turned and saw her staring at him. She did not try to disguise the fact. The concentration on his face softened, and he almost smiled. Almost.

Maria began to assess the place: the tiny kitchen, the barren living area with the lone wicker chair, the sloped ceilings; the golden bust of Elvis made her do a slight double take. When she finally absorbed the gray, plastic outdoor table and chairs, she recognized them.

"This was my father's," she said.

Mitch looked at the set. "Yes."

"I remember them. From when I was a kid."

"He lent them to me." A pause. "I'm a little short of furniture."

"It's the kind of thing that just sticks in your head." She reached out and ran a hand over the back of one of the chairs.

"I owe him."

The simple statement hung in the air.

She turned and walked into the entrance hall, retracing their earlier path into the two bedrooms, now seeing them with new eyes: the foam slab and sleeping bag in one room; the mattress on the floor, with blankets strewn about in the other.

The door propped across the sets of cement blocks, with the wooden fruit crate set in front of it as a seat, was clearly set up for a child. The *Mad* magazine, drawing paper and pencils that were scattered across its surface confirmed that. And when she saw the two other crates stacked against the wall, with a pair of small socks and underwear rolled up in one and a comic book in the other, there was no doubt.

She thought she was beginning to understand.

Then the purple stain on the mattress caught her eye, and she recognized it too. It had been her mattress, what seemed like a long time ago. She remembered vividly spilling the grape juice, and the hell that her father had given her as he had tried to scrub it out.

The memory was good, and alone in the room, she smiled.

She sat down on one of the gray plastic chairs. "You haven't lived here long, have you?"

"Not too long, no." He smiled wryly. "Is it hard to tell?" He pulled out one of the other chairs and sat down.

"A few weeks?"

"Something like that.

"How old is your little girl?"

Mitch was taken aback momentarily.

"That's her room, isn't it?" she asked.

He nodded. "She's nine."

"I was eleven when my parents got divorced."

"I know."

She looked at him. "You do?"

"Your father told me."

She pressed her lips together, then said, "Amazing."

"What?"

"That he would tell you that. He never talked about it. Not even to family."

Mitch slumped back more comfortably in the chair. "I guess he understood my situation, better than most."

"He must have liked you."

"I don't know if 'like' is the right word. I'm not an easy guy to like."

She thought of all that had happened in less than twenty-four hours. "You could be right," she said, and nodded. "You could be right."

My father had a place like this. A small apartment. Rented furniture. My parents separated when I was nine. The divorce took a couple of years." She looked upward. "I remember hiding inside the bottom compartment of this wall unit that came with the place. The whole thing tipped over with me inside it. Smashed stuff. Scared the hell out of me. And him. He gave me hell." She laughed abruptly, unexpectedly. "I was always getting hell for a while there."

Mitch listened, smiled.

"He was wonderful." She stopped, thought. "He suffered over the breakup. I could see it, even as a kid."

"He gave me good advice," Mitch said.

Maria looked at him.

"Told me he missed you till he hurt when he lived by himself."

She felt the feelings with no name begin to resurface, the ones that she had held down as best she could. It started in her chest, moved to her throat, then made her eyes watery.

"Said to go for joint custody, otherwise everybody'd regret it."

She let the feelings rise, float, let the river surging through her flood upward, let the waters that could not be held back any longer flow soundlessly down her cheeks.

"Said to make my daughter number one, and things would be okay."

He plugged in the electric kettle. "All I can offer you is coffee. Instant."

"Sounds perfect." She took a deep breath, then let it out slowly. The flood was subsiding, trickling back to hidden caverns. "What's your daughter's name?"

"Barbie. I just explained to her how babies are made. The experience made me age about five years."

Maria smiled.

He appeared to remember something. "I'm supposed to see her tomorrow." He frowned. "Things are a little confused right now though, aren't they?"

She nodded. "They are."

He thought for a while longer. Then: "Tell me about your studies. What are you doing? What comes next?" He took out two mugs from below the sink, began spooning in the coffee from the jar.

"Geography," she said. "Ph.D. work. Working on my dissertation."

He leaned against the counter with one hand. He looked at her like he hadn't really seen a woman in a long time. A pause. Then: "What's it on?"

She recalled the conversation at the dinner table with her father and Helen. "Madagascar."

"Madagascar? The big island near Africa?"

"At least you've heard of it. That's one up on most people."

"How'd you get interested in it?"

"Just one of those things. I've wondered about that a lot. How we get interested in things, I mean. Seems like some of it is pure chance, some of it a kind of inevitability. You know?"

"Yes," he said. "I do."

"Anyway, what I do is, I teach a couple of courses. I get some grant money. And I'm hoping next year to spend some time in Madagascar, doing field study for my thesis." She paused. "It's like another planet. Right now, I wouldn't mind being on another planet. A different planet from this one."

"Isn't that where you've been for the last twenty-four hours or so?"

She nodded. "Right," she said. "I have been." She continued to nod. "But there must be a gentler, saner one, somewhere. Don't you think?"

"I don't know," he said. "Sometimes, I doubt it. Sometimes I really doubt it." His eyes were unfocused. "But," he said, "I hope you're right."

"The Malagasies have a proverb. Gentle wisdom: 'Be like the chameleon: keep one eye on the future, one eye on the past.'"

The kettle began to boil.

Maria shut the door to Barbie's room and crawled across the mattress, dragging the covers up and over her. When her head hit the pillow, she closed her eyes, letting the exhaustion hit her like a wave. The rhythmic, deep breathing of sleep came quickly, but not before the comforting realization that she was back in her own bed, the bed her father had gotten for her.

She dreamt of red soil, golden lemurs, white orchids, and grape juice.

Mitch sat back in the wicker chair and closed his eyes. Sitting up, his chin on his chest, he dreamed of glaciers, of losing things he could not find, of rooms with no way out, and of the full lips of a woman's mouth. When he started awake an hour later, he was sweating and his heart was racing.

26

"Now is as good a time as any," said John Krygeri.

It was eight P.M.

Sam Karoulis lay in the hospital bed, a blanket and linen covering him to his neck. Wires and tubes ran from beneath the covers and from several placements on the skull to the brace of larger machinery beside him: in tandem were the Revival mechanism and its corollary computer.

The room contained Krygeri and Marcus—the doctors who had been there from the start—Helen and Maria Karoulis, and Mitch Helwig.

Krygeri's finger hovered over the switch.

Blue Limbo, thought Mitch Helwig. It's here.

Krygeri tripped the switch.

Who wants to try first?" asked Krygeri.

Mitch cleared his throat. "We talked about it. Both Helen and Maria agreed that I should try first. I want to ask him," he hesitated, his voice becoming noticeably raspier, "who killed him. That's all. After that, Helen and Maria can have him to themselves." A pause. "As they should."

"Fine." Beside the computer was a small table with a microphone and a separate speaker on it. The speaker had a set of headphones attached to it. Wires from the microphone and speaker ran to the computer. Krygeri motioned to the chair in front of the table.

Mitch sat down.

"A tape recorder automatically activates when the apparatus is turned on. By flipping this switch," Krygeri pointed to the one on the side of the speaker, "you transfer the patient's communication to the headset, allowing privacy. If you let the communication come over the speaker, you lose that. Which would you prefer?"

Mitch glanced from the speaker to the headset, then back at Helen and Maria. "In this case," he said, "we'll go public. If he can give us a name, a description, I think it's best if everyone in the room hears it, not just me. There'll be time, I trust, for private communications later."

"Go ahead, then."

Leaning forward, Mitch felt nervous, and shivered. Christ, he thought. An actual shiver.

The room was stone silent.

"Sam," he said, "It's Mitch."

There was a crackling from the speaker, as though atoms had been stirred by electric winds.

They waited.

"Mitch?" The voice was the computer's, and the inflection conveyed the question.

The silence was thunderous. Mitch's heart pounded in his ears.

Mitch cut to the quick. "Do you remember opening your front door, Sam? Do you remember who was there? Who shot you?"

The ensuing silence crackled with the static between the living and the dead. *"Where am I?"* came the response, filtered through the monotone of the computer's synthesis.

Mitch wasn't sure how to answer. The shiver transformed

into a visible trembling, and he felt Maria's hands on his shoulders, soothing, calming.

"Everything is blue," the computer's voice said. The crackle intervened. Seconds ticked by. *"I see,"* the voice said. *"I understand."*

Mitch's mouth was dry. It was too surreal. It couldn't be happening. His brain was reeling.

"Who shot you, Sam?" The words barked out and he gasped for breath.

The static reached an unearthly crescendo, the words careening through vapor, through electricity, through time, through infinite space. Then it was gone, and there was an unnatural clarity.

The single word came. *"Galecki."*

The static rose once more, crisp, biting, then muted to a soft stream.

"Joseph Galecki."

FOUR

We wake and find ourselves on a stair; there are stairs below us which we seem to have ascended; there are stairs above us, many a one, which go upward and out of sight.

—Ralph Waldo Emerson
Experience

27 When Joseph Galecki was thirteen years old, he committed his first break and enter.

His mother's house on Wolfrey Avenue, in the Broadview and Danforth area, was indeed modest: the middle one in an attached row of three, covered in insulbrick, containing two bedrooms and a three-piece bathroom; the floors of every room in the house were covered in an off-yellow linoleum. Joseph had his own bedroom and his mother had the other one. The only item that they considered to be a luxury was the twenty-one-inch black-and-white TV set, sitting on a chest of drawers in the living room, which had been turned on nearly every waking hour as long as Joseph could remember.

Thirteen had been an interesting age for Joseph—an awakening of sorts. Besides coming to terms with his new sexuality, he had pieced together many more things. Visits to friends' houses, movies, and even the constantly playing television set had begun to give him a larger frame of reference with which to gauge his life. He saw families that were much more varied and interesting than his. The fact that his mother never worked, and that he did not have—nor had never had as far as he knew—a father, was driven home to him simply by comparison. The very modest place that he called home came into clearer focus too as he saw how his friends' families lived, and he began to feel a sense of missing something that others took for granted. In one way it was a slow development, for it wasn't until he was thirteen that he began to realize that he was what was commonly called "poor," a word with the attendant social ranking that served to embarrass his adolescent sensibilities.

It was a warm and humid June evening when Joseph rode his bicycle across the Bloor viaduct and up into Rosedale to escape the television and the monotony of home. He had delivered newspapers in Rosedale two years earlier, and now, in hindsight, realized where he had been: in the leafy crescents and boulevards of the city's Old Money, where homes were stone or brick, where shiny cars were parked in garages as large as his house, and where there was never a hydroelectric meter beside the front door when you entered.

The lights from oak-paneled rooms shone out into the darkness as he glided by, the only sounds those of air-conditioning units in third-floor maid's quarters.

Lights from the other world.

He stopped in front of a house on Glen Road that he distinctly remembered from his days with the paper route. They had requested two *Toronto Stars* delivered—one to the front door, the other to the rear entrance. When he collected his money every second week, he was expected to go to the rear door, where the maid paid him his money. The interesting thing about it all was that it had made no particular impression on him at age eleven.

Now, it seemed to draw him like a magnet.

The other thing he remembered was that the people in this particular house told him that went away every June to their summer home in the Muskokas. They made a specific request to halt delivery of the papers for the month.

They were away now. Joseph knew it and could tell that the lights he saw were controlled by timers. He also knew that the TV tower at the back of the house could be scaled easily, and he could gain access via the roof and through the screen of the third floor's dormer window.

Joseph wanted to see inside. He wanted to see how they lived. He wanted to see the lights from the other world.

Inside, walking through spacious rooms and hallways, across hardwood floors, and into tiled bathrooms with showers and sliding glass doors, Joseph let the silence and solitude be his friend and mentor. To his amazement, it appeared that one room was allocated strictly for reading, its walls lined with glass bookcases, a huge mahogany desk at its heart; comfortable, thick rugs and cushioned deep, leather chairs. There was a billiard table in the basement and a sauna. He found a liquor cabinet that contained every imaginable shape and color of bottle. Framed paintings hung on the walls, some with small lamps shining down on them.

Until then, life had been a series of accepted routines, but things changed profoundly that night. In the long shadows of the house, he began to form his vision of what he wanted, of the comfort that he had been denied. On the third floor, he looked back out into the night through the broken screen that had been his entry point, and wondered for the first time where his father was.

That first night, he did not steal anything. Instead, he treated himself to a hot shower in the glassed-in tub, the first that he had ever had, draped the towel carefully back in its place when he had finished, and left the house with new, tangible goals.

That summer, he often strolled the shadows within the generous Rosedale mansions. They were his secret world. Sometimes he stole small items, sometimes not.

The hot showers were his favorite.

Five years later, he graduated with honors from Riverdale Collegiate, and immediately joined the Toronto Police Force. His dedication and work ethic earned him a steady stream of promotions as the years slipped by: within ten years, he had risen to staff sergeant; another five years saw him a staff inspector. The rank of superintendent was his next step, and six short years later he was one of the three deputy chiefs to the chief of police for the city. He often thought it would be nice to finish his career as chief of police, giving it a proper sense of symmetry.

He never married. Sharing his life, he felt, was not possible. There was too much that was beyond explanation to another human being.

And the nights of his youth, when he strolled the friendly, forbidden, interior corridors of the Rosedale privileged, remained at the core of his being. Indeed, he had continued the practice, in modified form, for several years after he had joined the force. It had always been quite clear to him that a policeman's salary, no matter how high he rose, would be insufficient to achieve the kind of lifestyle that he craved. There would have to be other sources of income.

It had taken him years to stumble onto what he felt was the right source.

Discretion was the key. The organization that had approached him had been discreet, and so had he. In return for handsome deposits in Cayman Island accounts, he became their facilitator. It was that simple. No overtly dirty work.

He bought the house.

It was on Glen Road. The very same house that he had entered that night when he was thirteen.

The dream was complete.

And then Mitch Helwig came along.

The organization had expected him personally to eliminate Helwig, along with Sam Karoulis.

Take care of it *personally,* they had said, and he had been allocated surveillance units. But to enforce their grip, to ensure that his dependability could not be compromised, it had been made quite clear that there could be no foul-ups. The message that was to be sent to anyone who had witnessed the Helwig–Karoulis warehouse coup was simply that they had paid with their lives. That was to be the observed price of such arrogant interference.

Deposits ceased being made in the Cayman Island accounts.

In his Rosedale mansion, stepping from the comfort of a hot shower, Joseph Galecki had understood fully.

28

"Sam. It's me. Helen."

The static crackled through the headset.

"Helen." A pause. *"I miss you."*

"They tell me we've got a few more weeks together. I think they'll be the best weeks of my life."

"What do I look like?"

She closed her eyes. "Like a young Greek god. Like you did when you were eighteen years old, with the fire in your smile and eyes." She opened her eyes and stared at him beneath the covers. "That's what you look like."

"It's like I'm in a room. A blue room. I can hear you, but I can't see you. I can't see anybody."

"How do you feel? Do you feel all right?"

The static, even, began to rise, then dropped. *"Strange,"* he said. *"I feel strange. I can't even see myself. Just blue."*

"There's nothing to see," she said. "I'm with you. I'm right here. Look," she said. He lay almost two meters from her. She did not move. "I'm scratching your head. The way you like. Can you feel it?"

The river of electricity bubbled and flowed. *"Yes,"* he said. *"I feel it."*

She smiled, grateful.

"I feel it," he said again.

It's me, Daddy. Maria."

There was the unearthly silence. Then: *"Madagascar,"* he said. *"You go."*

Her eyes began to flood.

The electric wind swirled in her headset.

"My little girl in a magic world. It's perfect."

There was no stemming the waters now.

"Perfect."

29 "I'm staying here, Mitch. With him. You go." Helen looked at Maria. "You too. Go. Get some sleep."

Mitch glanced at John Krygeri.

"It's all right," the doctor said. "We can set up a bed. It's been done before."

Mitch scanned the room, absorbing the feelings of those about him. Through the glass door he could see one of the replacement officers that Huziak had sent. He turned to Maria. "Let's go." He held out his hand.

With no hesitation, she took it, and they left.

What are those?" Maria indicated the two small black boxes that Mitch had placed strategically on the floor of his apartment. One faced the entrance door; the other was angled so that it focused on the skylight.

"Motion detectors." He stood up from the one he had placed in the entrance hall. "They'll let us sleep soundly."

Mitch had already swept the place for electronic bugs again. The apartment was clean. He wondered what someone was hearing from the one that he had tossed into the garden next door.

Maria looked directly at him. "Who is Joseph Galecki?"

"A deputy chief of police. You don't get much higher up."

"Is the name a surprise?"

He thought about it. "Nothing much surprises me any-more. But," he added, "nearly everything still amazes me." He sat down at the table. "Your father mentioned his name to me once before. Said that I was going to be suspended, and that the order would be coming from Galecki. Said that he thought he was next. So, if nothing else, it fits. It's always amazing though, what people will do to live the good life." He gestured toward his surroundings with a wave of his hand, indicating his vast wealth.

Maria managed a half smile. "What are you going to do?"

Mitch thought about his daughter, his father. "Tie up a couple of loose ends, then confront this Galecki."

"By yourself?"

The dark cloud came into his eyes. "It's usually better that way."

She looked at her watch.

"What time is it?" he asked.

"Eleven."

"Got no TV," he said. "Can't watch the late show."

Her eyes were tired.

"Have a bath. A shower. Crawl into Barbie's bed. Go to sleep. For tonight."

She began to rub her forehead.

"I'm going to do the same," he said.

She held her brow, not looking at him.

"No one will bother you," he said. He paused. "I'm used to being alone."

He had been asleep for about an hour when he heard his bed-room door creak open. In the dark, he opened his eyes, strain-ing to see.

"It's me."

Maria crept carefully across to the foam slab on the floor, kneeling down on it beside him.

"I'm used to being alone too," she said, "but not tonight."

He reached out and touched her shoulder, let her hair caress the back of his hand. She crawled into the narrow confines of the sleeping bag.

"Tonight," she said. "Just hold me."

She blended into his arms.

"Just hold me."

"Yes," he said. Their legs entwined and he felt her breath on his neck, soothing and regular.

"Yes." He squeezed his eyes shut and held her tightly.

In the darkness, in the warmth, they were finally able to sleep.

With sunlight streaming in through the window, Mitch woke. Still in his arms, inches from his face, was this woman, this soft wind that had touched his life in the most incredible way.

She opened her eyes, staring back at him. And in a gesture of kindness and honest affection, she kissed him briefly on the mouth, then slid out of the sleeping bag and left the room. Mitch watched her bra-and-panty-clad figure disappear, and when she had left him alone, he knew how much he needed to have her back.

30 "What do you think about, Sam?" Helen had taken off the headphones, listening to him through the speaker.

Photons gathered, crackled, then cascaded like the Styx down a steep cliff. *"You and Maria."* The crackling ebbed. *"What else is there?"* The electric river steadied, swirling more easily downstream. *"My mother,"* he said. *"I think about my mother. When she was young. Pictures I saw of her. How beautiful she was. Her hair, so black."* The stream eddied, turning lazily now, drifting in and out of shaded corners, over deep pools. *"My father. I remember going to see a movie with him. How rare it was. How excited I was. What his hand felt like when I held it."* It bubbled over small rocks, foamed white and black. *"My brother, whom I don't see much anymore. Whom I argued with."* A sudden pause, as if breath was being held. *"Whom I'll never see again."* The river widened, calmed, approaching an estuary. *"I remember pushing Maria on a swing in a park. It was March. The sun was shining. There was still snow on the ground. She was two years old. She was wearing her sunglasses, the world was so bright."* The photons blended into the electric sea, quiet finally, resolved into vaster depths. *"I remember everything,"* he said.

Alone in the room, Helen nodded.

"Everything."

* * *

Galecki," he said, *"is a fool."*

"We all heard. Mitch will take care of it."

"We're all fools."

"You're not a fool. No one can call you a fool."

"If," he said, *"I had another chance, I'd do some things differently."*

The crackling resurfaced, gently.

31 Sitting in the parked Chev across the street from Thorncliffe Public School, Mitch Helwig and Maria Karoulis finally heard the recess bell ring at 10:30 that morning. He watched carefully as the hordes of small children began to pour through the doors into the schoolyard. "There she is." She was with Lottie.

He stepped out of the car and crossed the street.

"Barbie!"

She turned at the sound of her name, saw him and waved. Running to the fence, she cried out, "What are you doing here?"

Lottie ran to join her, waving too. "Hi, Mr. Helwig."

"Hi, Lottie. Good to see you again."

Barbie was grinning widely. "Are you on your way to work?" she asked.

He shook his head and crouched down to talk to them. "Barbie, you have to come with me. Something important's come up."

She looked puzzled. "Now? I can't. It's recess. We're not allowed to leave the school grounds."

"It'll be okay. You'll be with me." He saw her hand clutching the wire fence and placed his own on top of it. "Lottie will tell your teacher, won't you, Lottie?"

The little girl smiled white teeth and nodded, happy to be an accomplice.

"Is something wrong? Something the matter with Mommy?"

"Nope. Nothing like that. I need your help, that's all. It's Wednesday. I was going to pick you up after school anyway, remember?"

She nodded.

"I'm just here a little early."

She thought about it. "Okay. I guess so." She turned to Lottie. "Tell Ms. Axworthy I'll do my spelling list tomorrow. Tell her my dad needs me."

"I will." She looked at the two of them enviously.

He stood up.

Still addressing her friend, Barbie said, "My dad needs a lot of help right now."

He smiled, looking at the two of them. Lottie met his eyes. "It's true," he said, and shrugged his shoulders.

Barbie saw the woman in the car's passenger seat as her dad opened the back door on the driver's side for her.

The woman smiled at her, and when she had climbed into the backseat, she held her hand out to Barbie. "I'm Maria."

Barbie looked at the hand, the smile, then reached out, letting her own small hand become enfolded. The woman's touch was warm, comforting, and Barbie smiled back. "Hi."

"I saw your room at your dad's place. A little bit of fixing up, and it'll be great." Maria was sitting sideways, her left elbow over the back of her seat.

The car pulled away from the curb.

"I had a room just like it at my dad's place when I was a little girl."

Barbie looked surprised. "You did?"

Maria nodded. "Yours is better though. Believe me."

Barbie sat back. "Where are we going?"

"To see Gramp," Mitch said. "He wants to see you. I think he's going to take you out somewhere for the day."

"Today?"

"That's right."

"Where?"

"We'll work that out when we get there."

"This sounds pretty weird to me."

"Sounds pretty neat to me," said Maria.

Barbie glanced from the woman to her father and back again. "Are you my dad's new girlfriend?"

Maria turned to stare at the little girl in the backseat, who had let a sudden smile overtake her after asking her question. Taken aback, an unbidden smile caught her as well.

Mitch half-turned to Maria for a moment, shrugged, then the smile became unanimous among them.

As calmly as she could, Maria looked at Barbie and said, "That's another one of those things we have to work out later."

32

When Paul Helwig heard the knock at his door that morning, he pressed the mute button on his remote, silenced the TV, and pushed himself up from the green chair where he spent most of his days.

Flo? he wondered. Mitch?

Two large men stood in the hallway when he opened the door.

The one on the left spoke. "Mr. Helwig?"

"Yes." He craned his neck upward.

"Do you have a jacket? We'd like you to come with us."

"Come with you where? What's this all about?" His irritation threshold seemed low this morning.

"It's about your son and granddaughter. They may be in trouble."

"I better tell—" The man on the right placed a firm hand on his arm as the old man turned to head back to the phone.

The man shook his head. "Can't tell anyone," he said.

Paul Helwig stared at him with weakened eyes. Then he looked down at the hand on his arm. The grip remained firm. He looked back up at the men without saying anything.

"Jacket?" the man repeated.

In a gesture of defiance and anger at his vulnerability, Paul Helwig jerked his arm free from the man's grasp, feeling his heart begin to pump his silent fear and rage through his aging body.

I was watching TV, you know." Sitting in the backseat of the moving car, beside one of his two escorts, Paul Helwig began to let his annoyance surface. "The Sandy Zwolinski show. It was about eunuchs. He had two of them on the show. From India. They said there were up to a million eunuchs in India, including transvestites, people born with sexual deformities, as well as castrated men. They had a two-day national conference to pick new leaders for the National Congregation of Eunuchs."

Neither of the two men paid any attention to him.

"Surprised you two weren't there," he said.

Where we going?" the old man asked.

No one answered him.

"Where's Mitch?" He was afraid to mention Barbie out loud.

Silence. They turned right at a stoplight.

Paul Helwig looked at the man beside him. "You've got too much hair in your ears."

The man glanced at him finally, a curious stare.

"They got statistics to show that guys with too much hair in their ears are prone to heart disease."

The man continued to stare.

"Combined with creases in the earlobes, the two can act as warning signs for coronary artery disease."

"You're a fucking nuts old man, aren't you?"

"Be a shame," Paul Helwig continued. "Nice fella like you. Feeling that big squeeze in his chest." He smiled defiantly back into the man's face.

33

"When you wake in the morning, with the whole day ahead of you, you think of yourself. You feel the blood coursing strongly."

Helen was holding coffee in a Styrofoam cup, letting it warm her hands.

"But then the evening comes. The day is done. You tire. Your family is around you. You stop being the center."

She watched the steam circle lazily upward.

"You lie in bed and think. And you become small again. There is so much to be done. So much hope, so much fear."

She tipped her head back, breathed deeply, knowing it was the easiest way to avoid a rush of tears.

"Are you there?"

"Of course. I'm right here."

The speaker began to crackle. *"You have to rule yourself. Not let circumstances rule you."*

"My Sam. You're becoming a philosopher."

The crackling waxed, waned, then stopped. *"I have a lot of time to think now."*

I have a secret, Helen." He paused. *"Everybody has a secret."*

"Keep your secrets, Sam. I don't need to know them."

"In my sock drawer, at the back. There's a metal box that my grandmother gave me when I was a boy. It's full of loons—dollars. I've

222

been dropping them in there for years. Last time I counted, there were more than six hundred of them."

Helen smiled, and her face quivered. "Big secret, Sam Karoulis. Who do you think's been putting your socks away all these years? Elves? That box isn't even locked." She collected herself, sighed. *"I'm* the one with the secret." She stared dreamily at the coffee cup in front of her. "I looked in the box." She paused. "I'm sorry."

"Give them to Maria," he said.

The static crackled steadily, softly.

"Tell her it's her passage to Madagascar."

34 When he rang the lobby buzzer for his father's apartment and no one answered, Mitch felt an eerie quiet descend into his brain.

Maria and Barbie waited patiently beside him.

He pressed it again.

Again, they waited.

Barbie spoke first. "What's wrong, Daddy?"

Another thirty seconds. He tried again.

"Daddy?"

"I don't know, honey." His head was starting to ring as adrenaline began to pump.

"Is there a superintendent or something?" asked Maria.

"There's a main desk on the second floor." He pressed that button as he mentioned it.

"*Yes?*"

There was a split second delay, then Mitch said: "Police. Open up." And he stared into the security camera's lens above them.

Mitch made a cursory check of the basement's health and woodworking facilities, as well as the laundry room, before returning to the main desk.

"He still doesn't answer, Mr. Helwig." The plain-looking woman at the switchboard met his gaze.

"You have a key, for emergencies."

Another woman, bespectacled and thin, had joined them now, leaving her own desk.

"Take us up there."

Maria and Barbie stood silently on either side of him.

In his brain, the molten steel was beginning to bubble.

The two women who had accompanied them seemed relieved to find the apartment empty.

"I wouldn't think there's anything to worry about," the plain one said. "He's probably just gone out for a walk."

Mitch looked around carefully.

The television set was still playing. His father liked things in order, no loose ends. He turned off lights when he left a room. It didn't ring right to Mitch that his father would leave the TV on.

He checked the closet. When he saw his father's cap and cane, he actually felt light-headed.

Mitch knew that he never left the building without them.

Flo," he said suddenly.

The others looked at him.

"He has a friend. Flo. He might be with her."

"Flo Springer?"

"I think that's her name. She's got an apartment two floors up. I was there once." He started for the door.

The others followed.

Flo Springer was just as perplexed as they were, and just as worried.

Standing with his back to them, staring out the window down onto Yonge Street, Mitch closed his eyes and tried to think. What was happening? Was he overreacting? What should he do?

He calmed himself. When he turned to face them, he realized how they were all depending on him to take the next step.

Me, he thought. It's up to me how many of us here might live or die.

And the thought made him angry.

And stronger.

Flo." He looked at her earnestly. "We need some big favors from you."

"Just name them, Mitch. I've got my first-aid kit in the bathroom." She smiled.

He took her hand. "I want Barbie and Maria to stay here with you for a few hours."

"It would be my pleasure." Flo squeezed his hand.

Maria glanced at him quickly.

"I need your help very much too," he said, turning to her.

"I want to help. Anything."

"Stay with Flo. Help her with Barbie." He paused. "Look after them."

Maria hesitated, then nodded. "All right."

"Don't answer the door for anyone but me."

A sudden silence met this statement.

"Understand?"

She nodded. "Yes."

For the first time, Barbie looked frightened. "What's happening, Daddy?"

"I have to find Gramp. He needs me."

"I'll put on some tea," said Flo, apparently sensing the need for routines and distractions. She scuttled into the kitchen. "Raspberry," she called back.

Mitch turned to Maria, took her by the shoulders and pulled her toward him, burying his head in her hair. He kissed her on the side of the head and whispered, "I need you more than ever now. Take care of Barbie. Remember—you two have a lot in common."

She drew her face back, stared at him, then kissed him. "I love you," she said. "Be careful."

He took strength from her words, and once again was grateful for the fate that had twisted her into his life.

Bending down, he picked Barbie right up off the ground and squeezed her tightly, kissing her on each cheek. She wrapped her arms around his neck.

"I love you, Daddy," she said.

"I love you too. More than you'll ever know."

Holding her, he felt his own life in her, and ached for any pain that she might ever know.

He left with the two women from the second-floor desk area.

"You have security cameras monitoring the doorways, right?"

"Yes."

"They videotape what they see?"

"Of course."

"I want to see this morning's tapes."

After ten minutes of fast-forwarding, he found it. There was his father, accompanied by two burly men, leaving through the front doors. The time registered on the tape was 10:21 that morning. Neither man was particularly recognizable or distinctive.

The plain woman and the thin, bespectacled woman sat beside him, taking it all in.

He turned to them. "Those two men took him. It's a long story. What you should know is that they had no right to take him. You should notify all your staff of this, and show them this tape. And," he added, "pay special attention to the security of Mrs. Springer and the woman and little girl with her. Understand?"

They nodded.

"Shouldn't we call the police?" asked the bespectacled one.

Mitch fell silent for a moment, then, his voice shaking, muttered, "I am the police."

They said nothing.

His heart filled with outrage. "I'll look after it." His blood pounding with fury, he left the two of them and went down the stairs and out the door.

The name Galecki floated in a red haze before his eyes.

 When the phone rang in Deputy Chief of Police Joseph Galecki's office, he answered it mechanically. "Yes?"

"This is the fire department, Mr. Galecki. There's a fire at your residence on Glen Road."

"What!" He punched the video button, but the screen remained blank. "Hello?" He continued stabbing at the button.

"You'll have to get here quickly."

The line went dead.

Still holding the receiver in his hand, he stared numbly into the static gray square in front of him. The cold frost of fear and wariness settled in his chest.

And as he headed out the door, an army of images and thoughts clashed against one another in his brain—all of them bad.

The front door of his house was wide open when he pulled up in front of it.

But he saw no signs of a fire.

A trap? In the middle of the day? Like this?

None of it made any sense.

He got out of his car.

* * *

The emptiness of the house puzzled and worried him as he went from room to room.

It was when he entered the library that he heard the voice behind him.

"This room looked sufficiently private."

He wheeled about.

Mitch Helwig was pointing a hand laser at his chest. "All these books," he said. "You must be a cultured gentleman." The door to the room clicked solidly shut behind him.

Galecki stood his place. "What do you want?"

"You don't ask who I am. That means you know."

The deputy police chief remained silent.

"You killed Karoulis."

"This is ridiculous. I don't know what you're talking about."

"How they ever got you to do it personally, I don't know. Clearly, they're much smarter than you. And just as clearly, you're into them for so fucking much that you can be moved like a chess piece."

"How did you get in here?"

"I'm a cop. Trade secrets."

Neither man moved.

"All these books," sighed Helwig, "and you're still fucking dumb. You should open them once in a while, instead of just having the maid dust them." He walked over to one of the glass cases, opened it, and slid a volume out. "I was browsing before you showed up. Wish I'd had a library like this when I was growing up. Wish my little girl had one like it too. But no, a piece of puke like you has it. All to himself." He glanced up at Galecki. "And no kids of your own, right? They might get your books out of order. Then you might have to kill them."

"You're crazy."

"I've been hearing that a lot lately." He held up the book in his hand, showing Galecki the title. *A Selection of Aphorisms.*

I'd like you to hear a couple of them before we proceed."

"Proceed with what?"

Helwig ignored him. He flipped the book open to where he had placed a bookmark, then set the book on the large mahogany desk, keeping one hand and eye trained on Galecki, holding the book's spine open with his other hand while he read.

"This is preposterous," exclaimed Galecki.

" 'If you wish to drown,' " read Mitch Helwig, ignoring him, " 'do not torture yourself with shallow water.' " He looked up. "An old Bulgarian proverb." When he elicited no response, he said, "See what you've been missing?"

Galecki was breathing deeply now, both anger and fear evident in his face.

"One more," said Mitch. He turned to the other marker in the book. " 'There is a certain satisfaction in coming down to the lowest ground of politics, for we get rid of cant and hypocrisy.' " Again he looked up. "Emerson," he said.

"This is madness."

"Yes." He nodded. "It is." He closed the book on the desk softly. "But this is the lowest ground. And we are about to rid ourselves of all hypocrisy." The laser had not wavered.

Then Mitch opened his jacket and focused the eye of the Barking Dog on Galecki.

The two men stared coldly at one another.

"You killed Karoulis."

Galecki did not answer.

"In these circumstances, silence is an admission."

"I don't know what you're talking about."

Mitch felt the stab of ice.

"And you kidnapped my father."

Galecki's eyebrows raised appreciably when he heard this. He repeated: "I don't know what you're talking about." But this time, the Barking Dog let it pass. The truth.

Mitch looked around the room, then back at Galecki. "Is this what it's all about?"

"I still don't know what you're talking about. I haven't understood anything that you've been talking about!"

"This," Mitch repeated calmly. "This room, this house, your furniture." He picked up a brass bookend from a shelf, turned it over in his hand, put it back down. "Creature comfort." He gazed at him piercingly. "You've got no family. No wife. No children."

"What do you know about me?"

"Police force is like a family. Lots of gossip." He shrugged. "Everybody knows you're a one-inch dick in Gucci loafers. Common knowledge."

"This is getting us nowhere. What is it that you *want*?"

Mitch Helwig put his left hand on the leather inlay of the big mahogany desk and spread his fingers apart. He lowered his voice until it cracked and rasped with a trembling, fierce passion. "I want my father back, you incredible piece of shit." His jaw clenched and unclenched, and white flares went off behind his eyes. The knuckles on the hand holding the laser turned to snow.

"I've never had anything to do with your father."

The truth.

"Who did it? Where is he?"

"I don't know."

The Barking Dog shivered, drops from an icicle.

Mitch raised his eyebrows. "You know something."

No answer.

"You're going to tell me."

Galecki licked his lips. "If you kill me, you'll learn nothing."

"Come over here."

Galecki hesitated.

"Now."

The deputy police chief moved to the far side of the large desk. Mitch was still leaning on his left hand, fingers spread apart.

"Put your left hand on the desk like mine."

Galecki frowned. "What?"

"Do it."

Tentatively, Galecki complied. He licked his lips again.

"Exactly like mine," said Mitch. "Fingers wide apart."

"What are you going to do? Torture me? You're not a sadist, that much I know." But the edge in his voice cut through to secret fears.

The two men leaned forward on their left hands, staring at one another.

Mitch Helwig's voice lowered once more into that manic area, and the raspiness made the hairs on Galecki's neck stand up straight. "I won't do anything to you that I wouldn't do to myself."

Mitch carefully aimed the Bausch & Lomb laser at his own left hand.

Galecki's mouth opened soundlessly.

Squeezing the trigger with a calm, steady motion, he burned a hole into the leather inlay with the cobalt beam, less than a centimeter to the left of his baby finger. The leather began to smoke and crackle.

Galecki's face tightened.

The white flares behind Mitch Helwig's eyes burst into a shower of kaleidoscopic sparks. "Watch," he whispered.

With a quick, deft motion, he cut off his own baby finger at the middle knuckle. His mouth opened and his head began to shake as the pain hit his brain in scalding waves.

"Jesus Christ!" Galecki started to straighten up.

Mitch quickly pointed the laser at the man's head. "Don't you fucking move, or I'll kill you where you stand." The tears began to stream down his cheeks.

"You're fucking crazy!"

Mitch looked down at the severed digit; even with the smaller vessels cauterized by the laser, blood still flowed freely from the larger arteries. Through clenched teeth, he said,

"You're absolutely right." And still shaking, he reached into his pocket with his left hand and brought out a white handkerchief, closing his fist on it.

They both looked down at the remnant of finger still sitting in a smear of blood on the desk.

"Fucking nuts!" shouted Galecki.

His head still shaking, Mitch said, "I wouldn't do anything to you that I wouldn't do to myself. Like you said: I'm no sadist." He gritted his teeth, letting the tears flow freely down his face.

He aimed the laser at Galecki's hand, still spread out on the desk.

"You can't cut my fucking finger off!"

"Yes. I can. Until you tell me what I want to know." He stared, blinking wildly and crazily into his opponent's eyes. "One finger at a time. Then toes, if I have to. First me, then you. Back and forth. Who knows where it'll stop?" The pain rolled off him in palpable waves. "Where is my father?" The breath wheezed out of him.

Galecki was literally trembling.

Mitch dropped his eyes to the man's hand. The arm clutching the laser was shaking uncontrollably.

"Jesus. Wait!"

Mitch waited, shaking.

"I can give you money." The tremor in Galecki's tone betrayed his attempt at control.

Behind the pain in Mitch Helwig's eyes, a new burst of white-hot madness blossomed. Whispering maniacally, he said: "You're from another planet." He shook his head. "Money . . ." He uttered the word as though he could scarcely believe what he had heard. "You want to buy my father." His eyes bored into Galecki's face. "And after I've sold you my father, what should I spend my thirty pieces of silver on first?"

Galecki was trembling.

"A big shiny car, like a pimp? A big house, like this?"

Realizing he had failed, the senior policeman began to

look around frantically, unable to bear the contempt in the
man's voice.

"Or maybe I should begin investing in furniture. Acquiring the right furniture is a worthwhile way to spend your life, isn't it? Or Royal Doulton china? Have my pattern registered at Birks?" he added, remembering Sam Karoulis's teasing. The hand holding the laser was steadying gradually. "You're a piece of human puke, Galecki. Looking at you, I see the putrid food chunks and smell the sour barf. How much should I sell Sam Karoulis's life for? What's the price of my self-respect?"

"I'm trying to buy my own life, for God's sake!"

Mitch nodded. "Of course you are. I never doubted it. That's all there's ever been for you." He spoke through clenched teeth, eyes blinking away the sweat that was running down his brow now. "Tell me what you know about where my father is. Tell me right now." His eyes dilated, white shot through with spiderwork veins of red. "I can't wait any longer."

Galecki swallowed, nodded. It was over, he realized. He couldn't stand against this man. He could only hope that by telling him what he knew, he might be spared. It was the only card he had left. "Down Cherry Street, past the Keating Channel. Turn onto Villiers Street. First street east is Munitions. On the corner is an old brick warehouse, painted blue. It's been the base of operations ever since they lost Herrington Storage last year." He looked at Mitch. "You know all about that."

"Is my father there?"

"I don't know. Probably. I don't know where else he could be."

The Barking Dog slept.

"Who's behind all this?"

"I don't know. It's like a multinational business. Layer upon layer. Numbered companies. I don't know."

Still the truth.

"It'll never end, will it?"

Galecki could not keep his eyes off the bloodstained handkerchief in Helwig's closed left fist.

"But you have to keep at it. It's like a disease. You keep trying."

"For Christ's sake, Helwig."

The laser shifted its sighting from Galecki's hand to his face.

"I've told you everything I know."

Mitch nodded.

"No heirs, Galecki? Do you have a will? Who are you leaving everything to? Who gets the Royal Doulton china?"

"Jesus, Helwig." He reached with his left hand to the ring finger of his right hand, slid off a gold, bejeweled band, threw it on the desk between them. "That's just the beginning. It's got a diamond setting. It's worth thousands." He was pleading now. "Let's work this out."

Mitch eyed the ring. "Everything is a deal to you, isn't it?"

Galecki waited.

"If I let you live, you'll just hire lawyers to carry on."

"Listen—" Galecki spread his hands apart, imploring.

"I'm not an easy guy to like," Mitch continued. "Sam Karoulis was. His family liked him too." He steadied the laser.

Galecki's eyes hollowed. His face fell.

Mitch squeezed the trigger. The blue beam erupted into life, joining the weapon's barrel to Galecki's forehead, burning instantaneously through skin, bone and brain. The man slid to his knees, then fell backwards, twisted unceremoniously on the floor.

Through tears and fetid smoke, Mitch Helwig watched the beam of light blink out of existence as he released the trigger, and he gasped for breath to fight the thunder and roar of his pounding heart.

He stood back for a moment, feeling slightly faint. On the desk, he saw Galecki's ring and his own finger, both lying in a pool of blood. Pocketing the laser, he scooped up the two items in his right hand, watching the dark red liquid seep through his fingers, staining the flesh.

My father, he thought. And Sam and Maria and Helen
and Barbie and me and a soldier in a glacier.

The blood was still warm.

He turned and left, closing all the doors behind him.

When he drove across the Glen Road bridge, he slowed,
opened his window, and hurled the finger far out into the
ravine below.

36 "You screw around with me or my boy, I'll put a curse on you." Paul Helwig stared brazenly up at the man leading him by the arm.

"We're already screwing around with you, old man. Sit down, and don't be so fucking nuts."

The older Helwig sat on the wooden chair. He was in a bleak room, inside a large warehouse, somewhere in the lakefront's industrial area, but his eyes hadn't been good enough to discern landmarks clearly from the backseat of the car.

Two more men entered the room.

Helwig spat contemptuously on the floor.

The men looked at him.

"Takes four of you weenies to hold me, eh? I curse the bunch of you."

They ignored him. From a cupboard on the far wall, they began assembling weapons.

" 'Death will slay with his wings whoever disturbs the peace of the Pharaoh.' "

One of the men chuckled, turning to Helwig. "And who are you? King Tut?"

"His minions were buried alive with him." He eyed the four of them, smiling.

"I don't like this Pharaoh stuff."

"For Christ's sake. Ignore him."

Each man adjusted the barrel and scope of a Sony laser
rifle, checking settings, removing safeties.

"Twelve of the excavating team died within six years of
opening the tomb. Dozens have died since," Helwig continued.

"What's he talking about?"

"He's crazy."

"I read about it," said one. "It was deadly spores, bacteria
that got loose. Curse, my ass."

"I don't like it. Let's shut him up."

"Relax."

"If this is to be my tomb," said Paul Helwig, sneering at
them, "you'll all be buried with me."

But he knew his smile was false bravado. It was Mitch he
was worried about, not himself. "Your eyes are all kind of close
set, aren't they?"

Two of them looked at him.

"I'll bet you weenies are distant cousins of the royal family."

What do we do now?"

"We wait. He'll come to us."

One of the men lit a cigarette.

Paul Helwig coughed. "Only a moron still smokes. Minister of Health says right on the goddamn package that you're
a moron. It's made you impotent, hasn't it?"

They ignored him. "You know what he did to the other
warehouse. Blew the fucking thing sky high."

"Not this time." He nodded toward the old man. "We'll
see him soon. If Karoulis told him anything, he'll go for
Galecki. Then he'll come here." He blew a smoke ring. "Alone."

37

"There's all kinds of rumors flying around, Mitch." Berenson, the force's mobile equipment manager, tucked his clipboard under his arm and leaned on the hood of the skimmer beside him. His glance kept returning to the white, bloodstained handkerchief covering Helwig's left fist. A few of the mechanics in the underground police garage had stopped working, wiping their hands on rags, eyeing the two of them, conversing quietly among themselves. "What's happening? Can you tell me?"

Mitch studied him, thought about it. "You deserve that." It was Berenson, after all, who had sent the Sikorsky to take Karoulis to Sunnybrook. "He's in Blue Limbo."

Berenson was silent.

"He's named Galecki. It's on tape. And Huziak knows where I'm going and why. He'll be down in a minute. I need thirty minutes' head start, then your backups can fly in. If I'm not out, Huziak will know what to do."

"Why you? Why alone? I don't get it."

"Huziak's doing me a favor." The storm rose in his eyes.

Berenson swung the door of the Honda prototype skimmer upward. "You've used this before, so I don't have to tell you much. More power and better handling than all previous air-cushion vehicles. And there's the CO_2 cannon embedded in the

front hood. And the vest." He handed Mitch the garment with
the four Semtex plastic explosive squares wired through it. "I
trust I'll get it back intact."

Mitch shrugged into it, then pulled his jacket on over top
of it.

Berenson noted the lack of reply. "And this." He handed
the flare to him. "Just pull the tab on the side if you want to
use it. But make damn sure your eyes are shut tight for fifteen
seconds. It produces five million lumens of light in one concentrated burst. Anyone looking at it will need several minutes
to regain full vision."

Mitch took it, put it in his pocket.

"Good luck."

Mitch swung into the seat, behind the wheel of the skimmer. "Thanks."

"See you soon."

Mitch just stared.

"Are you okay?"

The skimmer fired to life, rose thirty centimeters off the
ground, hovered, waiting.

Jesus, thought Berenson, as he watched him leave.

The last thing he noticed as the vehicle slid up the ramp
from the garage was Helwig's white-wrapped, bloodied fist
clutching the steering wheel.

38 "I like to draw," said Barbie.

"Well, then, I'll get you some paper and a pencil, and we'll see what we can do," said Flo. She rummaged in a kitchen drawer filled with string, paper, scissors, elastic bands.

"Have you known Mr. Helwig long?" Maria watched her from the living room, sitting beside Barbie.

She looked up, surprised. "Mr. Helwig? You mean Paul?"

"Yes. I guess I do."

"Long enough to know what I was missing before he showed up." She looked at Maria, one woman to another. "You know what I mean?"

Maria smiled, nodded, thought of Mitch. "Yes," she said. "I do."

"I know what you mean too," said Barbie. "He gives me two dollars every time he sees me. I've only managed to save eighteen dollars so far, but when I get enough saved, I'm going to buy a trail bike, with five gears." She fiddled with her buttons, watching the two older women carefully. "I hope Daddy finds him soon."

Flo stopped momentarily in sudden thought at the little girl's words. When the moment passed, she resumed her hunt. Finally, she pulled a large pad of paper and a pencil from the drawer. "Found them," she announced, and turned to see Barbie's tentative smile.

*   *   *

Well," said Barbie, "have you worked it out?"

"Worked what out?" asked Maria.

"You said you'd work it out later." She held a cup in place as she meticulously traced its circular bottom onto the paper. "Whether you were my dad's new girlfriend or not." She finished the circle, leaned an elbow on a knee and looked up into Maria's face.

Flo sipped her tea, smiled, pretended not to have heard.

Maria studied the innocence of the little girl's waiting eyes. "Would you like it if I were?"

The little shoulders shrugged. "Sure. He needs someone. He likes you. I saw him kiss you."

"Then the answer is yes." Maria held her breath.

Flo turned to watch.

"Neat," she said, and bent to her drawing once more.

39 The Honda police skimmer was still novel enough to turn a few heads as it glided east and south in eerie quiet into the city's gray area. The smaller ones had just about replaced the Harley-Davidson motorcycle fleet; there were only three of these, though, all still in the testing stages. The double turbine, the sophisticated mesh-gearing, the stabilizers that had been added to the corner thrusters, and the new horizontal tail planes all combined to let Mitch know that he was indeed riding a cushion of air.

He pressed the button on the dashboard, setting the gas-dynamic CO_2 laser embedded in the front hood on preheat and put on dark glasses to protect his eyes.

He turned left on Villiers and slowed as he reached Munitions.

Appropriate, he thought. What war had prompted the street's name? From the age of the buildings, he guessed it was the First World War.

His eyes took in the line of CP boxcars on rusted rails that hemmed the north side of the street, the decaying ramp of the Gardiner Expressway that faded down into Lake Shore Boulevard.

And then he saw the building. One story, painted blue brick, as he had been told.

He jockeyed the skimmer into a space beside one of the

boxcars across the street from the warehouse, parking it so that its front windshield faced the front of the building.

The preheat indicator on the dashboard blinked off. He flipped a switch. The sixty-millimeter cannon surfaced out of the hood.

With his bloodied, still wrapped hand, he opened his door, let it swing upward, and stepped outside, welcoming the throb and pain from what remained of his finger.

It's him. He's alone."

They gathered at the window to watch as Mitch Helwig crossed the street.

"He's got a fucking cannon pointing at us."

"His old man's in here. He's not going to do anything."

"We could kill him now, get the hell out of here."

"No. Let him come. Let's make sure. Besides," he said, "I want to see this guy."

"Eunuchs always want to see real men," said Paul Helwig behind them.

One of them turned to him. "You're an old man," he said. "Probably had a good life." He paused. "It's over today." He took a hand towel from a table on his way over to him, balled it up, and forced the old man's mouth open roughly, stuffing it in. Then he spoke to the other three. "So he can't shout out. I'll be in there. As backup." He nodded toward the room's other door, with a smoked-glass window. "I'll be able to watch what goes on in here without being seen. Cover you."

"Right."

Paul Helwig reached up to try to pull the cloth out of his mouth. Immediately, the man who had stuffed it there butted him in the back of the head with the rifle stock, knocking the old man's glasses to the floor.

"Leave it."

The old man's head spun in pain and dizziness, and a trickle of blood streamed down his scalp.

"Tie him up?"

"Just his hands. Behind his back."

The man left the room.

Paul Helwig felt small, helpless and humiliated sitting in the chair. And the probable truth of the man's words rang in his head.

It's over today.

When Mitch Helwig opened the door and stepped inside, he let his eyes adjust behind the dark glasses. He saw one man on either side of the room, and a third standing behind his father, who was seated in a wooden chair at the room's back center.

And then he saw the towel in his father's mouth, and the glasses on the floor at his feet, and the rage that had been bubbling all day, that seemed to have been bubbling for months, years, threatened to erupt like a geyser. But at the last second his father's weakened eyes met his, and the old man shook his head quickly, snapping Mitch back to what had to be done.

Coldly, he studied the room.

The two on the sides both had a laser rifle trained directly at him; the one behind his father had a similar weapon pressed against the back of the old man's head. He was the one who spoke. "Close the door."

Without looking back, Mitch reached behind him and pushed it shut.

You walk right in here. No weapon." The voice of the man behind his father was a quiet monotone.

Mitch held out his left hand, opened it, let the handkerchief fall to the floor.

All eyes were mesmerized by the tiny, bloodied half digit. Looped around the finger stump was a nylon cord that disappeared up his sleeve. "I jerk this string," he said, "and"—he opened his jacket carefully with his right hand, revealing the vest with the four Semtex squares wired through it— "we all go to hell together."

No one moved.

"You shoot me, they go off too. It's quite intricate. Besides this place disappearing altogether, there'd be a crater about two meters deep where it used to be." A pause. "I doubt if they could even identify us with dental records."

"This is bullshit." The observation came from the man to his left.

Mitch turned his head to him. "Try me."

"He's gonna kill himself and his father? C'mon."

Mitch continued to stare at him without answering.

The man with his father broke the silence. "So what do we do?"

"I take the vest off and put it on the floor. I get to hold onto this string though. You lay your weapons down. You send my father over here. I send him out the door behind me. Then I drop the string and leave."

Paul Helwig moaned something through his gag and squinted his watery eyes. The man behind him pressed the barrel of the rifle harder against his head, silencing him.

Mitch started, strained, then regained control. His eyes hardened to steel. "That's the deal," he said.

No sound.

Then: "All right."

An invisible wire seemed to stretch tight in the room.

Carefully, Mitch removed his jacket. Then even more carefully, he shrugged from the wired vest. With the nylon loop still around his finger clearly visible, he crouched down and set the garment on the floor, remaining in that position while staring at the man behind his father. "Now you," he said.

Time clicked by in slow-motion freeze frames.

While he waited, Mitch looked at what was left of his finger, white bone and red blood, poised to kill them all. He stared across at his father, eighty-four years old, half-blind, a towel jammed in his mouth. He felt his temples throb, a wave of nausea washing through him. The room, he realized, was filled with grotesque images, underscoring the meanness of life's sad underbelly.

The man behind his father set his rifle on the floor and straightened back up. Taking their cue, the other two did the same.

"Now. Send him here."

All eyes were riveted to the hand with four and a half fingers.

Without waiting, Paul Helwig stood up and stumbled across the room toward his son. Again, he moaned something unintelligible through his gag, and glancing into his face, Mitch saw fear, pleading.

But there was no time. Too many things could still happen. Mitch reached back and opened the door. "Get out. Now!"

The old man still hesitated, shouting from the back of his muffled mouth.

Deep down, in some primal crevice of his brain, Mitch understood that his father was trying to tell him that there was no deal, that these men had something set up to undo him, that they did not intend to let him leave there alive. And true as it may be, it still changed nothing. The only thing that mattered was extricating his father from this nightmare that was none of the old man's doing. He deserved that. It was the best that Mitch could do for him.

Their eyes locked.

Half-standing, Mitch spun his father around, pressed his good hand against his back, and shoved him forcefully through the door. When the old man lost his footing, and with his hands bound behind his back, tumbled onto his side, scraping his face on the cement, Mitch instantly buried the stab of heartache he felt. There was no time for it.

He slammed the door shut.

The men inside kept their eyes on what was left of the finger.

Behind the smoked-glass window, the laser-aiming system was silently screwed to the top of the thirty-centimeter-long black plastic barrel of the Sony. Then, carefully, the tiny red dot was sighted at the base of Mitch Helwig's baby finger where it joined the palm, just below the nylon loop of string.

Pushing with his tongue, gagging, Paul Helwig struggled futilely to rid himself of the cloth in his mouth. Then rolling over onto his face, he drew his knees up under his stomach, shoved back with his forehead against the ground, and raised himself to a kneeling position, his eighty-four-year-old heart pounding fiercely in his ears.

On his knees, bleeding, crying, aching, gasping for breath through his nose, all the pieces suddenly fell into place, and he saw what he had to do with a crystal clarity.

It was so easy.

There was no world left for him out here. It was all inside, back there. Mitch was the world he had created.

It's over today.

Almost joyfully, he embraced his life and his pain, an aching collage of memories: *his father's strength, his boyhood room, his mother's warmth, his beautiful bride, Mitch—his baby son—soft in his arms, his granddaughter's smile, Flo's healing touch.*

He stood upright, backed to the door, twisted the handle with hands still bound behind him, and pushed it open.

Then everything happened at once.

Mitch noticed the red dot on his hand only in the instant in which his finger was completely sliced off and the white-hot pain lanced his brain.

Paul Helwig forced his ancient body to run one last time,

past his son toward the door at the far end of the room. The laser that had been about to burn Mitch's life away swiveled toward him instinctively, cutting through his left arm and stopping at his heart, where it burned into his soul.

A mindless scream tore from Mitch's lungs as his brain tried to synthesize the chaos.

With sheer momentum Paul Helwig's lifeless body ran the three remaining steps, his upper torso crashing through the smoked-glass window before sliding, finally, to the floor.

Mechanically, his brain still boiling, Mitch wrested the flare from his pocket and pulled the tab. Closing his eyes, he tossed it into the center of the room, where the three men were scrambling to pick up their rifles, while he rolled laterally away at the same time. Instantly, the room went nova as five million lumens of light exploded in their midst.

Mitch squeezed tears from the corners of his tightly shut eyes, hearing, as if from a great distance, the shouts and cries of the damned about him.

My father.

The interim of darkness was a purgatory of horror, a black pool of limitless regrets, and his chest began to heave with uncontrollable sobs. When he finally, after the fifteen seconds had expired, squinted carefully through his dark glasses, he saw the blinded, stumbling men.

And he saw his father's crumpled body.

Already rumbling, the volcano inside him erupted.

With his head shaking and his mouth open in a soundless wail, he crawled to one of the laser rifles that had been placed on the floor, picked it up, pulled the trigger, and let the blue death beam cut through the three men with a single, ruthless sweep. Then he walked to the door that Paul Helwig had crashed into, looked through the shattered glass partition, saw the fourth man leaning blinded against the far wall. Methodically, he squeezed the trigger once more, and the blue bolt sprang from the mouth of the rifle like an angry god, boring relentlessly into his victim's chest, steaming his heart into a smoking, acrid vapor.

Only when the man fell forward onto his face did he release the trigger.

And then he knelt and gathered his father into his arms, held him, and wept with a grief he had never imagined existed in his whole life.

Mitch carried him to the skimmer and placed him in the passenger seat. Then he got in behind the steering wheel, reached across and put his arm around him, drawing him near, holding him again.

Blue Limbo, he thought.

And he thought of Karoulis. The wires. The tubes. Of Helen, Maria, Barbie, Flo.

No. It was over. It was time to let go. Paul Helwig would prefer it that way. He kissed him and straightened him, buckling him into the seat. Taking care of him.

Then he gazed through the windshield at the blue-painted brick warehouse, sighted along the length of the laser cannon, donned the night-goggles, and pressed his thumb down on the activator. The thick shaft of light that burst forth blazed into the front door, disintegrated it, then found the vest with the Semtex and the whole building went up in a deafening blast of spectacular oranges, yellows and blues.

He held his father's hand and waited for the police copters to arrive.

 Mitch set the mugs of instant coffee on the gray plastic table in front of Maria. "You leave next month?" He touched her neck.

She sipped the coffee, nodded. "The twelfth."

"I'll miss you."

"Everything's changed since I made my plans. I don't want to leave."

"It's only six months." He sipped the steaming liquid. "I'm used to being alone, remember?"

She smiled.

"I'm not going anywhere. I'll be right here." He reached into his pocket, put something in her hand.

"What's this?" Maria turned the gold ring with the array of diamonds inset on it over in her fingers. She looked at him. "It's a man's ring."

"Sell it. It's yours. Use the money for Madagascar."

"I can't take this."

"It's not mine."

She frowned.

"It belonged to a man who owed a debt to your father. I'm just passing it on. It's yours now."

Maria stared at him, then at the ring.

Is there a heaven? A hell?" The questions surprised Mitch even as he asked them. He didn't know where they came from.

The fifth floor unit was deathly quiet. Mitch was alone with Sam at last.

The electric crackle grew, waned, as he reached into Blue Limbo.

"No." Then: *"I don't know."*

A tremor.

"I thought it might have become clear to you."

The stream of electrons spread into quieter tributaries.

"Many things are clear to me," Sam Karoulis said. *"The things that matter."*

"What should I do?" Mitch asked. He could feel him slipping away. He could feel everything slipping away. "What should any of us do?"

The static built, then burst delicately.

"Forgive," Sam said. *"Everybody."*

They're going to let me go today." The voice in the headset was followed by the electric crackle.

"I know," Mitch said.

"Time," he said. *"It's the enemy."*

Mitch said nothing, just listened.

"Blue Limbo is over."

For you, thought Mitch.

For you.